A Candlelight Ecstasy Romance®

"FACE IT, CALE. IT'S NOT THAT YOU JUST DON'T CARE FOR COMEDY—YOU DESPISE IT! AND SINCE I'M A COMIC, YOU THINK OF ME AS A CLOWN, A FOOL!"

"Don't take it so—"

"Stop trying to shush me." The words came out in a near wail as Sandy began to feel the true depth of her misery. "Just leave me alone," she said in a choked voice.

"Come on, Sandy, I'm sorry I hurt your feelings, but—"

"Hurt my feelings?" Now she couldn't stop the tears. "Is that all you think you did? You blew away my whole career with one remark, and you made it clear that we can't have a relationship."

He paled a little, but he said, "You're going to push this all the way, aren't you? You want me to crawl."

"The only place I want you to crawl is out of here and away from me."

CANDLELIGHT ECSTASY ROMANCES®

354 SECRET INTENTIONS, *Jean Hager*
355 CALLING THE SHOTS, *Kathy Alerding*
356 A PRIVATE AFFAIR, *Kathy Clark*
357 WALKING ON AIR, *Michele Robbe*
358 RELENTLESS PURSUIT, *Eleanor Woods*
359 SENSUOUS ANGEL, *Heather Graham*
360 WORDS FROM THE HEART, *Natalie Stone*
361 INTERIOR DESIGNS, *Carla Neggers*
362 TOMORROW AND ALWAYS, *Nona Gamel*
363 STAND-IN LOVER, *Barbara Andrews*
364 TENDER GUARDIAN, *Cathie Linz*
365 THE TEMPTRESS TOUCH, *Lori Herter*
366 FOREST OF DREAMS, *Melanie Catley*
367 PERFECT ILLUSIONS, *Paula Hamilton*
368 BIRDS OF A FEATHER, *Linda Randall Wisdom*
369 LOST IN LOVE, *Alison Tyler*
370 SO MUCH TO GIVE, *Sheila Paulos*
371 HAND IN HAND, *Edith Delatush*
372 NEVER LOVE A COWBOY, *Andrea St. John*
373 SUMMER STARS, *Alexis Hill Jordan*
374 GLITTERING PROMISES, *Anna Hudson*
375 TOKEN OF LOVE, *Joan Grove*
376 SOUTHERN FIRE, *Jo Calloway*
377 THE TROUBLE WITH MAGIC, *Megan Lane*

ALWAYS KEEP HIM LAUGHING

Molly Katz

A CANDLELIGHT ECSTASY ROMANCE®

Published by
Dell Publishing Co., Inc.
1 Dag Hammarskjold Plaza
New York, New York 10017

Dell ® TM 681510, Dell Publishing Co., Inc.

Candlelight Ecstasy Romance®, 1,203,540, is a registered
trademark of Dell Publishing Co., Inc., New York, New York.

ISBN: 0-440-10331-2

Printed in the United States of America
First printing—November 1985

For Chris, Terry, and Carolyn,
with all my love

To Our Readers:

We have been delighted with your enthusiastic response to Candlelight Ecstasy Romances®, and we thank you for the interest you have shown in this exciting series.

In the upcoming months we will continue to present the distinctive sensuous love stories you have come to expect only from Ecstasy. We look forward to bringing you many more books from your favorite authors and also the very finest work from new authors of contemporary romantic fiction.

As always, we are striving to present the unique, absorbing love stories that you enjoy most—books that are more than ordinary romance.

Your suggestions and comments are always welcome. Please write to us at the address below.

Sincerely,

The Editors
Candlelight Romances
1 Dag Hammarskjold Plaza
New York, New York 10017

CHAPTER ONE

It wasn't going to be a terrific Saturday night—Sandy had known that as soon as she'd left the West Side Highway and found the city as quiet as an owl at high noon. She hated these steamy summer weekends. Sometimes it seemed people moved to Manhattan just to become prestigious enough to leave it regularly. She was raring to do a hot set tonight, and where was her audience? Sniffing each other's Bain de Soleil in the Hamptons.

She found a parking spot on East Seventy-first and headed for Twinkles. Not only was it muggy; a hot wind kept gusting up, swirling street grime around her. As she turned the corner onto Third Avenue, her earlier impression was strengthened: it was definitely not going to be a great night. Outside the club about a dozen of her fellow comics were gathered, as they usually were while they waited to go on. But tonight they weren't clowning around and trying out new material on one another. They were being harangued by a street character. Sandy couldn't make out his words from a block off, but he was probably raving that the world would end Tuesday, or aliens had landed in Central Park.

She skirted behind everyone, hoping to get inside

the club without attracting the pest's attention. But his words began to register—and she realized he wasn't a loon at all.

"Why can't you people honor a simple request?" the man demanded. "I've asked you several times not to crowd the sidewalk like this. Caleb's is my property, I like to keep it looking decent, and my customers shouldn't have to fight their way through you to get to my door."

Sandy stopped and watched him. Not the tallest man she'd ever seen, but he sure was one of the best built—strong, solid legs planted authoritatively apart on the heated pavement, shoulders beneath the crisply tailored suit jacket so massive that your eye didn't think they were ever going to stop. His face, flushed now, looked as though it would be quite nice in calmer moments—gray eyes, very like hers, dark hair trimmed fashionably short. Warm-honey tan, boyish chip in a bottom tooth.

She made herself focus on the man's words. If he had a beef with the Twinkles comics, that included her. What was his problem? Now that she looked again, he was more belligerent than authoritative. The tan was probably a Hamptons special, and the haircut—each strand individually sliced at Bergdorf's, it would have cost nearly as much as the suit, which hadn't come from Woolworth's. . . .

"—inside! Why do you have to hang around out here, crowding a public street? It's just plain inconsiderate!"

Sandy was getting the idea. He owned a place on the block and objected to the nightly sidewalk antics of the Twinkles bunch. That was somewhat under-

10

standable. Their whistling-in-the-dark horseplay did get noisy. But to accuse them of harming his business, whatever it was—that was too much.

Nobody was talking back to him. Everyone was studying their toes or the heat-hazed night sky. We're so used to being dumped on, Sandy thought. Well, she, for one, wasn't going to take this. She hadn't inched her way to the top of the beehive in a showcase club by letting herself be walked on.

"Excuse me," she said, stepping forward. "Aren't you making an awfully big deal about a minor problem? All this noise because a few performers like to come out and enjoy the night air. Don't you have anything important to worry about? Who are you, anyway?"

He'd been trying to rein in his temper. But this woman's hostile words didn't help. She seemed to be attacking *him*.

"I'm Cale Fowler," he said. "See this place?" He hooked a thumb at the club next to Twinkles. "Caleb's. That's my real name. I own it. It's a music room. Music *only,*" he said meaningfully, looking from one comic to another before going back to Sandy. "People who work at my club are musical artists, the best jazz and pop singers in the business. No sleazy rock groups. No punkers. Certainly no *comedians.*" He spat the term as though it were *child molesters.* "My customers come to a nice room to watch a dignified performance. They don't need to be annoyed by these characters howling like banshees on the sidewalk." His eyes pinned hers. "*I* think that's important enough to worry about. *You* can go enjoy the night air in hell." He turned,

11

banged open the door to Caleb's, and stalked through it.

"Don't beat around the bush," Sandy called after him. "Tell us how you really feel!"

There were a few uneasy chuckles, but the others looked as jarred as she felt. Years of facing tough New York audiences had helped Sandy develop a tortoiselike cover, a thick dome that protected her. But there was something about this man, something about those eyes that drilled through her shell as though it were Saran Wrap. And his barbed words had jabbed right through as well, hurting, surprising her with their power.

"Isn't he the one who might buy Twinkles?" asked Brenda Cass, another comic.

"Oh, is that story going around again?" Sandy said. "About once a year there's a rumor that the club is being sold. Virgil probably starts it to keep us in line."

"I don't know," Brenda said. "This might be more than club-owner machinations. Maybe he'll sell if he can get enough."

"I heard this place is really bothering Fowler," said Marcus Brawn, an impressionist. "Not only doesn't he like Twinkles people hanging around outside, but—you'll love this—he complains about the laughter filtering through. Is he serious? If we got enough laughs to penetrate a wall and interrupt a singer in the club next door, we'd be in Vegas."

"One of us does—and she'll be there any day now," Brenda said. "Sandy just got back from a gig in Denver. How was it? Can they breathe easily enough to laugh up there?"

12

"It went well—better than tonight looks like it'll be," Sandy said. She wanted to go inside where it was cool, start getting the feel of the audience.

Brenda went in and Sandy moved to follow, but a motion off to the side caught her eye and she turned. Cale Fowler stood in his doorway. She tensed, wondering whether he was coming out to make more trouble. But he came no farther.

Why did he just wait there? Maybe he couldn't decide whether to start in again. Was she imagining that he looked directly at her?

No. And if she wasn't still so mad at his arrogant treatment of her and the others, she might even enjoy gazing back at him. He *was* attractive, when he wasn't all bunched up with anger . . . his arms folded instead of gesturing angrily.

He let his eyes drop slowly to look at all of her, and Sandy thought, Okay, Charlie, and began her own perusal. She was pleased to see discomfort unsettle his tanned features when he realized she was looking him up and down as frankly as he examined her.

Then she was staring right into his eyes. Those are for walking barefoot through, she thought, caught by their intense silver-gray opacity. Break the connection, Sandy. . . .

She spun away and stood facing the rushing Third Avenue traffic, collecting herself.

Marcus touched her shoulder. "Is it my breath?"

Sandy laughed. "Just out to lunch for a minute. Who is that man Fowler?" She looked back at Caleb's, but now no one was there. "Where did he come from? I've only been gone a week. He appeared out of nowhere."

"The way I heard it, he's owned the place for years, along with another music room on the West Side. He managed that one and his partner ran this. But the partner wanted out, so Fowler bought his piece and sold the other club."

"And he might buy Twinkles too?"

"So they say."

"Why? Just to get rid of Twinkles? Or does he really want it?"

"Don't know." He peered at her. "Your face is dripping. Did you get used to that Denver altitude already? Or don't you feel well?"

She pushed her tight curls back and palmed sweat from her brow. The night wind blew dirt at her face. The evening hadn't even begun, and she felt as though she'd done two shows to a roomful of dull-normal hecklers. Why did the image of the rude man next door keep returning—and why did her neck prickle when it did?

"I feel fine," she said.

"Really? I'm Mahatma Gandhi."

"I thought I knew that turban from somewhere. No, honestly, it's just the heat. Let's go inside."

The air-conditioning was a delicious assault after the muggy sidewalk. But as she made her way to the women's dressing room to repair her face, Sandy had to admit that the weather wasn't the only reason she'd wilted like yesterday's lettuce. That opalescent gaze . . .

Forget it. You have two sets to think about.

Empty, thank heaven—she had the dressing room to herself for a precious few minutes. She could cool down, regain her composure. If she went onstage like this, she'd bomb. Once that audience sensed you weren't in the driver's seat, it was all over.

She stood, arms hanging, chin up, feet apart. Deep breath, slow exhale, deep breath, blow out. Mmm, better. Her five-seven frame, cheetah-slim, wore the posture proudly, lissome legs straight, modest but shapely breasts uptilted. Her clothes reflected the look she liked for performing—easy to move in, roomy, with just enough pizzazz to remind her and anyone else who might wonder that she'd turned in her copywriter uniform years ago. Creamy trousers fell over her hips in pleats; above a chain belt her rust blouse was woven through with gold threads. The colors brought her red-blond hair alive. It was layered into longish wavelets, a cut that was supposed to tame it, but it had swollen to masses of tiny curls in the July humidity.

She blinked at her reflection, her long, pale lashes shining gold in the fluorescent light. Okay, we're getting there. Between the air-conditioning and the relaxation technique, her face would no longer scare little children. Some more blusher, a touch of highlighter to con the world into believing she had cheekbones . . .

Conning the world—that must be my mission in life. This is my second career in it, Sandy thought. If I'm not pushing peanut butter, I'm pushing patter.

She'd spent eight years climbing the rungs in advertising so she could sock away money while raising Dan decently, working a regular schedule.

Then, when she felt he was old enough—and that, at twenty-eight, she'd be *too* old if she waited longer —she'd decided to stop being clever on someone else's payroll and put her wit on the line. The *real* line—the one that didn't let you josh yourself. In front of an audience you were good or you weren't; they bought you or they clobbered you with indifference.

When she'd quit she was a highly paid writer at a hot agency, no small deal even in a city where every third person at the Bloomingdale's lunch counter was a big-ticket executive. She'd been ripe for a chief spot, and a vice-presidency before long.

But in a matter of weeks she'd gone from wool suits to jeans; her workdays began at nine P.M. instead of A.M. as she went full-time into stand-up comedy. She performed free at all the showcase clubs, did everything she could to learn. For the next six years her personal life, every part of it but Dan, had run a far second.

Now, at thirty-four, Sandy knew she was out of working-your-way-up chips. She'd risen in comedy to the point she'd reached in advertising. This time she had to make that leap over the edge, to the next level of success. Bigger and glitzier gigs, more national TV appearances.

She fluffed her curls with her fingers. Bits of hair around her face were damp—she'd just have to hope they dried fast. Virgil would no more have provided a hair dryer in the dressing room than a Picasso.

What a difference between that world and this one, she thought. Ready to be a copy chief . . . I

16

wasn't sure I could stay awake long enough to make it. But this . . . this is like being on a *cliff.* The high of blowing away a room on a good night—there's nothing like it. The power . . . the control. I'm the one in full charge. It's the most exciting thing on earth.

Finished with her repairs, she leaned into the mirror. Was her energy up, attitude locked in? She tried to see herself through the audience's eyes. Would you buy a used joke from this woman?

Nine-thirty. The band was playing, the show starting right on time. It usually did on weekends, since there was a second show at one. The crowd wasn't as bad as Sandy had feared, fortunately, because she was up second—first comedy spot, following a singer. That was fine, if the emcee warmed the audience properly. Otherwise she'd need to use half her twenty minutes playing with them before she could do material.

As if reading her thoughts—which would have been one for Ripley's, since he was as perceptive as a toaster—Virgil came up behind her and said, "You could do a long set if you want."

Sandy turned. His round face radiated unintelligent good cheer as he waited for her to thank him for the "favor." His offer told her two things: the performers' lineup was sparse tonight, and the reservations were even more so.

He'll never head the physics department at Stanford, Sandy thought, but he's shrewd. He knows I won't need to salaam to him much longer. He's getting his strokes in now, so I'll recall what marvelous fellow believed in me when I was too green to make a hyena laugh.

"That's sweet of you," she said. She crossed her fingers behind her back, the part of her that loathed dishonesty unwilling to be trampled entirely. "I'll pass, though. I want to try out some new stuff, but I don't know about the room." Not to mention that the other performers might come after her with machetes. She remembered how it felt to be lower on the totem pole and watch some star go on and on, leaving you a raunchy audience you couldn't handle.

"Anytime," Virgil boomed, clapping her back with a chubby paw, choosing to treat his gesture as magnanimous even if she didn't.

She turned to the stage. "Where you from?" Marcus Brawn asked a man at a front table. As emcee, he was starting to work the audience, bringing them in, extracting what laughs he could. "They're having a conference to decide," he told the room as the young man whispered to the woman with him. "And what answer have you and your wife decided on, sir? *Is* that your wife, by the way? Or is this a business trip?" He knew enough not to wait for responses. He looked around for better meat and settled on a large group to the side. "Let's see where these guys are from. We'll start with the smokers because they don't have as much time. . . ."

After ten minutes the audience was laughing easily. They felt at home now, eager to be entertained. Marcus had done a good job, and Sandy was grateful. Her set would be that much more relaxed.

The singer did three numbers, ending with a nice

up-tempo one that left the right mood. Marcus introduced Sandy, kissed her cheek as she strode onstage. She stood for a minute, smiling, surveying the room. She always liked to start slowly. No comic could sustain the energy produced by a firecracker barrage of lines up front, and she preferred to build gradually, letting them buy her attitude, know who she was, laugh with the way she saw things.

"Any out-of-towners? Let me tell you some fun things you can do in New York. Bank tellers here have a great sense of humor. If you want to give them a good laugh, walk into Citibank with a stocking over your head. They'll love it. Oh, and if you're tired of partying, if you want a quiet night watching TV, just go into any bar on Eighth Avenue and change the channel from the Yankee game to *Falcon Crest*. Nobody will mind."

She was doing well. She had them. The set was half over and she was coasting along, setting up jokes and knocking them down with dry punchlines. Her concentration was total, though she appeared to be just chatting breezily.

A movement by the entrance pierced her focus, and she turned her head. Caleb Fowler had come in —and stopped just inside the door, leaning against the wall with his hands in his pockets, his expression unreadable. He looked as though he intended to stay there awhile.

Angry that she'd let him interrupt her flow, Sandy forced herself back. But she'd looked at him a beat too long, distracting herself and the audience. She was expert enough to pull their attention back, but her rhythm was broken and she had to finish on automatic pilot.

She ended to applause that was more than polite but less than ecstatic. Cale was still by the door and when she glanced at him, he motioned her over with a nearly imperceptible gesture. She considered ignoring it. Who was he that she had to obey when summoned?

But she was more curious than annoyed. She made him wait a minute while she busied herself with the tape recorder she used for every set; then she began threading her way through the side tables to him. He didn't try to meet her halfway. He leaned arrogantly against the wall, his hands in his pants pockets, which kept his jacket open and the trouser fabric stretched across his fly—a pose that, Sandy suspected, he well knew was tantalizing.

Finally she reached him. "Can I help you with something?" she asked frostily. "You seemed to be trying to get my attention."

A frown flickered across his brow and he straightened. "I came to see you. To apologize."

There was nothing but sincerity in his face now, and Sandy was abashed. She realized he'd simply been waiting with polite patience, not arrogantly forcing her to come to him. She could handle nastiness; courtesy turned her to jelly. How dare this infuriating man behave so unpredictably when she'd been all set to deal with more of his peevish temper? For probably the first time in six years, she stood speechless. "Uh . . ." she began helpfully after a long silence.

He waited for her to go on, his face expectant.

I should be committed, Sandy thought frenziedly. Tell me to drop dead and I'm brilliant, they give me the Pulitzer. Be nice to me and my brain gets up and leaves.

"Maybe we should—" he began.

"No, it's . . ." she jumped in, determined to produce an intelligible sentence. The noise level was climbing as Marcus introduced the next act and the band played him on. Her words hung in the smoky air, then eddied away as she realized how interesting Cale's face was and cocked her head to study it. Cheekbones you could do a swan dive from . . . wide, expressive, well-defined lips . . . eyes the same pearly gray as hers, but with dark lashes instead of pale . . .

"How did you chip your tooth?" she asked before she knew she was going to, then dropped her head in embarrassment. Why don't you just *tell* him you're a moron, Sandy, and save him the bother of finding out for himself?

He grinned, spoke; his reply was lost in a spatter of laughter in the room.

Sandy leaned close to his ear. "We could talk better outside." She smelled no after-shave, only sweet, clean skin and freshly washed hair. "That is, if you think your customers can fight their way through us as we crowd the sidewalk," she couldn't resist adding.

He grasped her hand and led her through the door. Outside the air was still so moistly heavy Sandy felt as though she could grab a handful and fling it, but the relative quiet was a relief. The racing, weaving traffic with its squeals and honks was a soft symphony after the sound system at Twinkles. They walked past the door to Caleb's and stopped by an alley between the club and the next building.

"I have a tendency to bite off more than I can chew," Cale said.

"Excuse me?"

"You asked about my tooth."

"Oh." She would have preferred to forget that question. "Did it take you all this time to come up with that? I'm glad you don't try to do this onstage."

He started to answer, but there was a gust of hot wind. He gasped and bent his head, his hands going to his eyes.

"What's wrong?" Sandy asked.

All she heard was a soft noise of pain. He moved one hand, revealing tear streaks.

"Cale? What is it? What can I do?"

He sniffed. "Contact lens."

"Well, take it out."

"Not it—both. Some junk must have gotten in my eyes."

She stood, feeling sorry for him, not knowing what to do.

"It should wash away in a minute," he said, sniffing some more. "About that apology . . . I guess I just wanted to say . . ." He stopped. His eyes were streaming harder.

Sandy wanted to cry herself. He was so clearly in agony but trying to be brave. She said, "You've got to take them out. Let's go inside."

But he'd already had enough pain. He was removing the lenses, switching hands awkwardly, since he had to hold one while popping out the other. He raised his head. His dark lashes were matted into spiky clumps, his face dripping.

"Thank heaven," Sandy said. "You look better already. Half drowned, but better. Can you see?"

"No."

"You really can't?"

"I really can't," he said a bit too sharply. "I can hardly function without these. That's why I didn't want to take them out."

"Can you clean them off in your mouth and put them back in? I could hold one while you try."

"That never works for me. I have cleaning stuff in my office—"

"Well, then . . . ?"

"The office is in the back. I can't go stumbling through the club with my lenses in my hand. There's a door off the alley, but—look, I hate to ask—"

"Ask anything," Sandy said, feeling worse for him every minute. "I want to help."

"Okay. You can help by getting that door open. It's a killer." With his empty hand he pulled keys from his pocket and gave them to her.

Sandy started down the alley.

"Wait," he said. She turned. "You'll have to be a German shepherd for a minute. Walk next to me, okay?"

Sandy gaped. "Good grief, you can't even see that much?"

"Not without light. I don't want to trip over something and drop these. The alley is always full of

23

garbage. There's everything but an aircraft carrier down here."

He was right. Bottles, cartons, and other obstacles unidentifiable in the dark littered the narrow space. They went slowly. Once she had to move fast to kick aside a broken flowerpot; she'd been so distracted by his fine profile, even more attractive than he was full face, that she'd almost missed it.

They reached the door. "It takes two hands to open it," Cale said. "Ready?"

She was admiring him again. She wasn't prepared for the question. "What?"

"Are you ready to open the door while I tell you how?" he asked patiently.

"Oh. Sure." So far he's seen me bungle what could have been a nice set, and then forget how to work my vocal cords to produce words, Sandy thought. It's time I showed him I can accomplish something. "What should I do?"

"See the keyhole there, under the knob? It's hard to find in the dark."

She bent, located it, and inserted the key. "Okay."

"Now turn the key left and hold it there while you lift the doorknob with your other hand—lift it hard—and pull. Got that?"

Any other time it would be no problem. Right now I might as well be trying to break into Attica. What is this man *doing* to me?

The door wouldn't budge. She turned to consult Cale and found his face inches from hers. The perspiration that had until now merely beaded demurely on her forehead and upper lip became unladylike sweat. She wiped it away, hoping he couldn't see, and tried again. She turned, held, raised, and pulled, but the door didn't give.

"No luck?" Cale said.

"No." Her palms were damp and sore.

"Let's try together. I do have one good hand."

Holding his right hand safely out of the way, he pulled on the knob while Sandy held the key. For one insane moment as they struggled, she wished the door would never open, that they could spend the whole night right here, his breath a little ragged in her ear—maybe not just because of the exertion? —the roughness of his jacket teasing her arm and shoulder through her diaphanous blouse.

Then suddenly the door was open, and welcome cool air enveloped them.

"This way," Cale said. In the light he could see well enough to lead her down a corridor. She followed him into a small square office. He snapped a light switch and she saw a single window that probably overlooked the alley. A metal desk faced the door; on it were a black phone, two neat stacks of papers, pens and pencils. A threadbare settee and two hard chairs completed the decor. Nothing adorned the walls but a few cracks and holes in the plaster.

This room didn't look as though it was inhabited by the same man who wore those clothes and that haircut with such familiarity. Sitting down, Sandy groped for a diplomatic way to say so. "Looks as though you're just moving in," she said finally, remembering what Marcus had told her.

He chuckled. "I am. Thanks for your tact. In

thirty-nine years I have learned to use a dustcloth, actually—I just haven't gotten to it in here. Not that it'll help much. I think my ex-partner's taste in furniture fell somewhere between Goodwill and condemned."

He was fumbling in his desk drawer with his free hand.

"Can't I help?" she asked.

"Nope—got it."

He pulled out a bottle of solution, cleaned his lenses, and put them in. He blinked to position them. Watching, Sandy felt the odd sensation of looking into her own eyes—lenses and all.

"I wear them too," she said.

"Contacts? No kidding. Hard ones?"

"Soft. The permanent kind. You only have to take them out every couple of weeks to clean them. And if a cinder gets in, it doesn't feel like a dinosaur."

He nodded. "I've been thinking about getting those."

Silence fell, not a comfortable one. Cale went to the settee and sat next to Sandy. The air between them hummed with electricity. She wondered if he felt it as piercingly as she did.

"I still haven't apologized," Cale told her, his intense gaze holding her. "You weren't as polite as you could have been, but I shouldn't have responded that way. I overdid it. I hope you'll forgive me."

Sandy's eyes opened wide. "Not as pol— You treated me like a bag lady!"

"That was after *you* were so hostile. And I didn't

26

mean to insult you personally. I was mad at all of you. I'm sorry."

"*I* was hostile?"

"Look, I said I was—"

"At least I didn't tell you to go to hell!"

He leaned back against his corner of the couch and put his hands behind his head. His shirt wasn't even damp. And the beautifully cut clothes fit his hard-looking body without a tuck to spare.

"Want to tell me now?" he asked, grinning.

Sandy sat back in her own corner, resisting the urge to fluff her blouse to create a breeze. In here it was much cooler than outside, but for some reason she was still terribly warm. All her clothes felt wet.

"Actually, I'd rather ask you something," she said with all the dignity she could summon. "The word around Twinkles is that you're looking to buy. Is that true?"

He frowned; hesitated. "Maybe."

"Why not give me a straight answer?"

"If you mean why don't I give you a definitive yes or no, it's because nothing is settled yet. What I think you're really asking is, Why do I seem uncomfortable discussing this?" He smiled slightly. "If you knew how pugnacious you look asking me these questions, the answer would be obvious." She didn't return the smile. This leggy lady with the hair like curled sunshine was tough to thaw. He went on, "That's all I can tell you. Nothing is definite."

She took a deep breath. "And would there still be comedy at Twinkles if you owned it?"

Gray eyes met gray eyes for a long moment. "No."

"Damn you," she said through clamped teeth.

He stood and paced the small room. Frustration chewed at him as he tried to understand. "I don't see why this is such a big deal. There are so many showcase clubs and cabarets in town. Sandy Shaw can write her own ticket at any of them. All the owners know who you are—you do network TV, you're booked out of town a lot, you're going to make it. Why should one dive more or less make a difference to you?"

She was surprised that he knew so much about her—and delighted. She squirmed, fighting the feeling, determined to see this vital issue through.

"You don't understand comics very well, do you? Having a home club is terribly important. Sure, I can work the other rooms; I do them all. But at Twinkles I get up there and take right over. I'm so used to the room, I know its dynamics without needing to think. When I want to try new stuff, that's the place. If someone is coming to see me—whether it's press, or a TV producer, or an agent booking a gig—that's where I'm most comfortable showing what I can do. Losing it would be a big blow."

"Well," he said, sitting next to her again, "you probably don't need that security as much as you think, a hot act like you. There's such a thing as too much security for a performer, you know. It can make you overly comfortable, keep you from reaching out. But nothing's settled, so it's too soon to worry."

"With me it's never too soon. Worrying is my hobby." She saw him blink with difficulty. "Are those bothering you again? You really ought to think about soft ones."

"I guess you're right. By the way, you were nice to help. If you hadn't been with me when I had to take the lenses out, I might have lost them. I don't know how I would've gotten home. Let me thank you properly. What would you like to drink?"

"Um," she said eloquently, needing a minute to recover. When he said "thank you properly," she'd thought he was going to kiss her. Her heart had thumped before her head had processed the rest of the question and she realized she'd completed it out of her fund of dialogue from old movies. "Uh, would a vodka and tonic be too much trouble?"

"Of course not," he said, going to the door. "Dave!" he called down the hall. "Please bring two vodka tonics. And an onion loaf." He turned back to Sandy and noticed her face was moist. "Is it too hot in here? I can turn the air-conditioning up."

But can you turn yourself down? she asked silently. She couldn't shake the fantasy image of Cale leaning toward her on the couch, touching her lips with his wide, soft ones. . . .

"It's fine," she said, searching madly for a topic of conversation. She should have declined the drink and left. "Couldn't you have taken a cab home?"

"Pardon?"

"Your lenses," she said desperately, fresh sweat popping out on her brow.

"Oh. No, I don't live in town. I live in Westchester County. It's about twenty-five miles—"

"I know," she said, surprised. "I live there too."

"Really!" He looked disproportionately pleased.

Maybe he shared her delight in the rare occasions when one discovered that not all entertainers were vampire-pallid urban creatures. "I'm in Tarrytown, near the river."

Sandy smiled. For some reason, she couldn't stop smiling. "We're ten minutes apart. I live in Hastings. I commute every night."

"By train?"

"By little red Honda."

Cale, too, seemed unable to stop smiling. They were still grinning at each other when a knock sounded and a waiter gave Cale a tray. He handed Sandy her icy glass with its tang of lime.

A delicious aroma wafted from a napkin-shrouded basket on the tray. Sandy glanced lustily at it. "Hungry?" he asked, holding the basket out to her.

She lifted the napkin and had to stop herself from plunging into the steaming loaf-shaped mound of fried onions with both hands. She'd forgotten he ordered it—and that was the craziest thing that had happened all night. To have forgotten about food because of a man! Sandy Shaw, the appetite with arms and legs!

"And what are *you* having?" she asked, clutching the basket possessively.

He chuckled and sat beside her. His direct gaze almost made her lose her appetite again. He really *looks* at me, she thought with wonder. He doesn't talk to my left shoulder. She was so sick of the ego-bloated nightlife types who talked over, around, through, and at her. She could be a fireplug.

They shared the onions, pulling the crisp strands

apart, and finished their drinks. Sandy checked her watch. It was almost twelve, time to go back to Twinkles for the second show. She stood, brushing onion crumbs from her lap. Though patches of silence had been so easy while they shared their snack that she hadn't even noticed them, now she felt awkward again. This man left her with no aplomb, she who could hold full control on a New York nightclub stage.

She glanced around, waiting for guidance. Should she use the side door, or go out through the club itself? Cale's fingers circled her upper arm. She turned to look at him. He was about her height, and their heads were suddenly very close. The effect was tantalizing, as if they were lying down facing each other.

"Thanks for the drink and the onions," she said, trying to ignore the arrows of heat where his fingers were.

"I enjoyed your company," he told her, leading her down the hall to the side door. "Neighbor," he added, smiling.

She smiled back, reluctant to leave, wishing he'd say something about seeing her again.

He unlocked the door and she stepped out. "You won't mind encouraging your—uh, colleagues to go back indoors if they're on the sidewalk, will you?" he asked.

Disappointment knotted her belly as the import of his words sank in. Had this all been a ploy? Give the lady a drink, a bite to eat, and a few seductive glances, and she'll do your bidding?

She'd really thought he was very . . . he'd

seemed so . . . but yes, she could see the whole routine now: she'd been stupid to think Cale wasn't just another showbiz operator out for number one. His act was a little more polished, that was all. Oh, he probably liked her well enough; the man was just keeping his priorities straight, taking care of business.

Cale seemed to know from her face what was going through her mind. "Sandy, I didn't mean that the way it sounded." He tried to make a joke, head her off. "If you didn't know me better, you might think I just wanted a security guard."

"Know you?" she asked icily.

"Well, yeah. We certainly know each other better than we did, say, yesterday."

"And as well as we're going to, say, tomorrow."

"What do you mean?" he asked. This was getting away from him. One marginally dumb remark, and she was treating it as a capital offense.

"I mean," she said with grim purpose, "that I don't see why I should spend any more time with a man who only wants me for one thing." Her face colored. "I don't mean the usual one thing."

He started to reach for her. "Well, I could arrange—"

"Oh, that's such a copout." She spun away in disgust.

"Will you make up your mind?" he shouted, his patience wafting away on the hot breeze. "Am I a villain who's using you to unclutter the sidewalk, or a villain who only wants to ravish your maidenly body?"

"Maybe whichever! Maybe it doesn't matter, as long as you can use me for something!"

Now disgust was on his face. "That's a cruddy thing to say. Did anyone ever tell you you have a short fuse? Not to mention barnyard manners. It's a good thing I'm *not* asking you to police the Twinkles bunch. You don't know what decent behavior is in the first place!"

"Is that what you think? Fine. I sure wouldn't want to do anything that might prove you wrong. So I'll just make it a point to block the sidewalk as much as possible. If there aren't enough people to make a nice ruckus, I'll hire some. Then you can come stomping out of Carnegie Hall here and make an even bigger fool of yourself than you have already, raving like a maniac. *Neighbor!*" she yelled over her shoulder as she stalked down the alley. Behind her, she heard a rattle, a creak, and a slam as Cale went back inside.

CHAPTER TWO

Sandy's late set went well, but it was surprisingly hard to maintain her attitude. She'd trained herself to perform no matter what her mood, and she was used to going onstage after arguments and upsets— but this business with the man next door had her in turmoil.

She packed up her tape recorder and said her good nights, forcing her attention to the drive home. She was determined not to let this stupid thing bother her further. She jogged around the corner onto Seventy-first, her keys already in her hand. In a few minutes she'd hit the West Side Highway; the Hudson River breeze would refresh her. As she bent to unlock the door, she realized the Honda was sitting at an odd angle.

She stepped back, puzzled. The curbside tires were flat!

Sandy slammed the side of her fist on the car's roof, winced, did it again. She needed this like another navel! How she loathed being helpless, under the control of anyone or anything else. Two thirty on Sunday morning, the last train had left an hour ago—and she hadn't the haziest idea how to change a tire. It was one of those things she'd always meant to learn, like baking bread. Besides, she had only one spare.

She heard a toot and looked up. Caleb Fowler, at the wheel of a gleaming black car longer than Idaho. How infuriating! If she ever wanted to see the man again, which she didn't, it wasn't when she needed help. Please, God, take him away and bring someone else to rescue me. Anybody. Virgil. Charles Manson.

"Trouble?" Cale asked softly.

"Why, no. I always stand around in the middle of the night staring at my car instead of getting into it and driving away."

He craned his neck to look up the street, then back the way he'd come. "You have a problem," he said, still using that quiet tone, "and I don't see a large selection of helpers around. I'm it. So I'll be a forgiving guy and give you one more chance. Would you like some help?"

"Yes," she mumbled, head down.

"What's that?" he asked, so loudly that she jumped. "I can't hear you."

"Yes," she said louder.

"Say it so I can hear it."

"*Yes!*" she shrieked.

"Shh, you'll wake the whole neighborhood," he said, getting out. He stooped and examined the Honda's collapsed tires. "Slashed," he pronounced, probing the rubber.

Sandy groaned.

He stood and brushed off his pants. "Face it, Her-cules—you need me. In fact, you're lucky I'm here.

How else would you get home to Westchester at this time of night?"

I won't answer that, she thought sullenly as she walked around his car and got in. The interior was even more luxurious than the exterior. Carpeting you could lose a small animal in. Lighted panels of numbers that told you the temperature inside the car, outside, and what it would be in your uncle's condo next week.

"What kind of car is this, anyway?"

"You're welcome," he said, his eyes on the road.

"Oh, sorry. I appreciate this."

He glanced at her. "You mean it?"

She glanced back. Why should he care? But he did, she could see. Maybe she'd condemned him too quickly before.

She yawned. Two sets, two—no, three encounters with this frustrating, interesting, confusing man. It had been a long night.

"Yes," she answered finally, and the word came out stretched, contained in another yawn. She snuggled back against the tufted upholstery and felt drowsiness begin to swallow her. She was asleep before they reached the parkway.

A hand was patting her shoulder and she smelled honeysuckle and skunk.

"Sandy," Cale said softly, "we're in Hastings, but you have to tell me where you live."

She opened her eyes and sat up, looking groggily out the car window.

"I got off the Saw Mill Parkway at the first Hastings exit, but now I need directions," Cale said.

She oriented herself and told him the way. Quickly the events of the evening clicked into her memory. She'd gone to town on a quiet Saturday night, ready to work. She'd found a man shouting at her friends, and had defended herself and them in her usual hair-trigger fashion. But the man had turned out to be very appealing and sexy—and then, after getting her interested, had let her down, one of the usual types after all, sensitive as a rubber boot. And had been the only one around when she was stuck on East Seventy-first Street with two flat tires. Glad to help, though she'd blasted him a couple of hours before.

Cale was pulling up in front of her house, a stone cottage with woods in back. He cut the ignition but she knew that only because she saw him turn the key. The engine barely made a sound.

"What kind of car did you say this was?" Sandy asked, covering a yawn.

"I didn't. But it's a Lincoln. Do you like it?"

"It's lovely. And so comfortable," she said, feeling remorseful. She could have been in deep trouble; she should be thankful he'd been there. But instead she'd been nasty—and then had rudely fallen asleep! "I'm sorry I wasn't awake long enough to enjoy riding in it."

"This doesn't have to be your only chance."

She started to speak, stopped, and sighed.

"You're still wondering if I'm using you, is that it?" he asked gently. "Or part of you is wondering, anyway. Look, I . . ." He paused, abashed by her frank, open gaze. Her face was so lovely, fair even in

37

July. Her skin had the smooth flawlessness of the inside of a shell.

"What is it?" she prompted.

Cale was finding himself suddenly bashful. He couldn't let her go like this, still suspicious of his motives. But how to make her see . . . ?

"Do you think—I know it's late, but maybe I could come in a minute? Just for a cup of tea?"

"I'd like that," she said, "but I'm afraid not. I don't want to wake my son."

He sat up straight. "You have a child?"

"Hardly a child. Dan's fourteen. He looks down at me and has chest hair."

Cale's face held amusement and admiration. "Very interesting," he said slowly. "You don't look old enough."

"I'm not," she said through another yawn. "I don't think I ever will be. Adolescent boys are impossible."

"So you and Dan live here by yourselves?" he asked with elaborate casualness.

She burst into soft laughter. "No, Helen lives with us. She keeps house and takes care of Dan when I'm working or out of town." She swallowed a final chuckle. "I'm sorry for laughing. That question was so earnest—it made me feel nice. Like you really care whether I'm taken."

She saw him relax. "So you're divorced."

"Yes," she said. "For ten years now. You too?"

"No. I've never been married."

"Why not?" she asked unhesitatingly.

Her directness caught him off guard. "Just . . . never wanted to enough, I guess. But you're right—

38

I do care whether you're taken," he said, emboldened by how she seemed now—softer, easier to talk to. "That's why I wanted to come in. To explain things."

"What things?" Her voice had a cool edge. Was *he* taken?

"You don't miss a beat, do you?" he asked, jarred yet again by her quickly parrying question.

She shrugged. "If you don't ask, you don't get answers."

"Well," he plunged on, determined to ignore her mercurial mood changes and say his piece, "I wanted to make it clear that no matter how it seemed before, I was *not* being nice to you to get your cooperation. You weren't being used. I'm not in the habit of manipulating people and I certainly wasn't doing that tonight." He leaned toward her. His eyes pinned hers. "Do you believe me?"

She was quiet for a long minute. "I think I do," she said finally. She stepped out of the car, then ducked her head back in. "Thanks for the ride. You saved me. Maybe I'll get a chance to pay you back." She closed the door—it ticked shut with almost no sound—and went up the walk and into the house.

She slipped off her shoes and walked barefoot down the hall to her room. Helen had turned off the air-conditioning and opened the windows to let the fragrant night air fill the house, but she'd forgotten Sandy's room. She raised the double windows opposite her bed and leaned her elbows on the sill. The night sounds from the woods relaxed and comforted her.

She undressed and climbed into bed, calm enough

to sleep but still confused. For six years she'd single-mindedly pursued her career, dating occasionally, rarely having a real relationship. She hadn't avoided entanglements; the temptation just hadn't been there.

And was it there now? She stretched under the fresh sheets. Maybe. She hadn't met a man this interesting in a long time. Cale was sexy, perceptive; he seemed to care what she thought and felt. Most men she met through her work only cared what she thought of their chances for making the Carson show.

Then again, she hadn't come this far in comedy by diverting her energy. Hadn't she spent a lot of it on Cale in just this one evening—enjoying him, then questioning his motives, getting mad, and back around the maypole? She knew she overreacted to any threat of rejection; it was part of why she did comedy, and paradoxically, part of what comedy had done to her. That fear had been operating at full throttle tonight with Cale. Plus, she could see already that some things about her made him uncomfortable.

So ta-ta, Mr. Caleb Fowler. Your onion loaf is divine but you're leery of me and I'm leery of you. Let's stay out of each other's hair.

And yet, as she sank into sleep, she had the nagging feeling that wasn't what she wanted at all. . . .

"Mom?" Dan was saying from her bedroom doorway in a whisper louder than most people can shout.

Sandy struggled up from sleep. "Morning, love. What time is it?" she asked fuzzily.

"Ten. I know, I know," he said as she closed her eyes and groaned. "I wasn't going to throw ice water on you till eleven. But there's a guy here."

She sat up abruptly, her red-gold hair tumbling around her face in curly wisps. It couldn't be. It must be a repairman, a salesman. But this was Sunday . . .

"Did you see his car?" she asked, remembering the black Lincoln.

"Yes," Dan said, puzzled. "It's red. A Ford, I think, or a Mercury."

Sandy felt a curious combination of relief and disappointment. "Can't you take care of it, Dan? At least find out what he wants."

Dan sighed, his postpubescent patience ebbing. "I already know what he wants. He wants to see you. His name is Mr. Fowler—"

She gasped and jumped out of bed. "He told you that?" She ran to the closet, then to the dresser.

Dan followed her zigzag route with his eyes. "Of course he told me. How else—"

"Right, obviously. I'm an idiot." She opened a drawer, rummaged in it, slammed it shut. Pull yourself together, Sandy. Someone who drops in without calling just has to cool his heels, that's all.

"He'll have to cool his heels," she mumbled to herself.

"Okay." Dan left the room, closing the door.

"Wait!" she yelled. She yanked the door open. "Dan!"

He came back down the hall. "What?"

41

"Don't tell him that!"

"Okay," he said bewilderedly. "What's the big deal?"

"No big deal. Offer him coffee or tea, then either make it or break the news to Helen that she has to. Then just talk to him for a while."

"What do I talk about?"

"The Yankees," she said, heading for the bathroom.

"I don't know anything about the Yankees. Besides, I have to leave in five minutes. Dad's picking me up."

"So turn on some music. That's it—music. Talk to him about that until Dad comes," she said, closing the bathroom door.

Twenty minutes later Sandy emerged from her room feeling imperfect but presentable in a khaki skirt and soft yellow T-shirt. Nervously she started down the hall. What was he doing here? Why hadn't he called first? And how could he be up and functioning so early? Her own eyes felt as if she were blinking over gravel, and she must have had more sleep.

She reached the living room just in time to hear Helen calling from the kitchen to a perplexed Cale, "Feenished beg?"

"Pardon?" Cale shouted back.

"Beg. I get," Helen said, bustling in. Sandy watched Cale look on in astonishment as Helen inserted two sturdy and apparently heatproof fingers into his mug and withdrew the tea bag. Then she carried it back to the kitchen, oblivious of the fact

42

that it was leaving tawny drips on the pale blue carpeting.

Cale suddenly noticed Sandy standing at the entrance to the room. His eyes narrowed with pleasure as he surveyed her lithe form in the brief skirt and snug T-shirt. His expression grew a tiny bit less shell-shocked.

"She's Ukrainian," Sandy said.

"That clears everything up."

"She must have adored you on sight. Otherwise you'd have been lucky to get a glass of water. Helen hates to work."

Cale looked at her blankly. Well, at least something is too much for him at this hour, Sandy thought. Getting dressed certainly wasn't, though. His pewter polo shirt made glossy gray lakes of his eyes, and the crease in his white slacks could have sliced a roast.

She joined him on the couch, leaving a sedate cushion's width between them. "This is a nice surprise."

"Did you think I'd leave you stranded?"

Sandy stared at him. What was he— Oh, the *car!*

He watched confusion turn to awareness in her face. "You must be doing even better with your . . . entertaining than I thought," he said. "Not everyone can afford to discard a Honda like a piece of Kleenex." He moved to set his tea mug on an end table, and the muscle in his bare upper arm rippled enticingly. "Or is it that you're so rattled by my presence, you can't think straight?"

She yawned hugely. It happened to be involuntary, but it was a perfect response to his arrogant teasing.

"So you're either tired or bored," he said. "My ego picks tired."

"Your ego's correct. How can *you* be that wide awake after so little sleep?"

He shrugged. "Comes with the turf. You should know that as well as I do."

"I do know it, but my body doesn't. Well," she said, settling back against the couch, "I guess you've rescued me a second time." The man really was a work of art. The idea of being clasped in his powerful arms thrilled and even frightened her a little. And the intellect in his eyes, the sensitivity of the face . . . cheekbones she'd give anything for. Why did men always get them, not to mention the eyelashes? It all seemed too good to be true. Which probably meant, a clearheaded voice reminded her, that it was. But she couldn't help the tremor of delight that shook her as she remembered being close to him last night in his office, in his car . . . the delicious aroma of his skin . . .

". . . find the listing," he was saying.

Her gaze, which had drifted, snapped back to his. "Sorry. Say that again?"

He eyed her curiously but repeated, "I would have called to make sure you were up, but I couldn't find the listing. Do you keep your number unpublished?"

"No, but it's under my real name, Shoresky." So that was why he hadn't called. Of course. Did you expect him to *divine* your name, you dingbat?

"How come you changed it?" he asked.

"Oh . . . when I first started on the circuit, I thought it was too long, ethnic, and unpretty. So I called myself Sandy Shores. To sound like a stripper. It took me months to realize it sounded more like a retirement community. Anyway, when I started to learn the ropes, I decided gimmicky names were dumb. You're inherently funny or you're not. But I didn't want to lose what little momentum I had as Sandy Shores, so I picked Shaw because the sound was close."

"But why did you want your name to sound like a stripper's in the beginning?"

She shrugged. "It led into some material. Since I'd be such an unlikely stripper, it was easy to joke about."

"I don't understand why you'd be an unlikely stripper. Because of your personality?" He looked genuinely bewildered.

"My personality!" She laughed. "What does that have to do with it? I didn't know strippers had to take aptitude tests."

"Well?" he pressed.

"I don't have the body for it, obviously."

He shook his head slowly, incredulous. He stood and moved over to her, grasped her under the arms, and pulled her up. Now they were face to face, their mouths only a kiss apart; but he stepped back, motioning her to stay where she was.

She stood still while he examined her, transfixed by his interest. Her limbs felt languid, rubbery. She missed the closeness of the moment when he'd lifted her; wanted to feel him that near again.

His eyes burned a trail of heat along her body,

moving from the tightly curled strawberry cascade down over the narrow waist and smooth bare legs, to the slim feet in beige sandals, the nails painted coral. Then he started upward again, only to stop and linger on the rounded breasts outlined by the shirt. For a long, bold moment he kept his eyes there, so smolderingly intent that she felt as if it were his fingers on the heated flesh. Desire simmered way inside her and she could see in his face that he knew it; knew she wanted him to hold her and that he wanted to.

But it was the wrong place and hour. Sandy pulled herself back to reality with an effort. She could sense Cale doing the same.

"I know you're funny because I've seen you work," he said, sitting on the couch again. "But I don't need any more evidence than I have already to know you'd make a fantastic stripper."

She chuckled nervously. "I'm too old to change careers again."

"Good, because I only want private performances."

She swallowed. Every time she tried to get the conversation back on an innocuous track, he said something that inflamed her again.

"Would you like more tea?" she asked hopefully. Maybe if she had a reason to leave the room . . .

"No, thanks, I haven't even started on this yet. I was distracted." He smiled at her, lifted the cup from the table, took a sip. And made a face of such disgust, he might as well have swallowed Drano.

"That bad?" Sandy murmured sympathetically.

"Worse," he said, setting the cup down as though

46

it might explode. "What can a person do to hot water and a tea bag?"

"I don't know, but Helen always manages. You should taste her coffee."

"Oh?"

"If you can imagine the water in which have been boiled the socks of the entire Ukrainian army after it's marched through Russia . . ."

"I get the idea." He stood. "Ready to run into town? You won't have to drive back here without fortification, of course. I can see it's up to me to get you a decent pot of coffee. How about brunch at Tavern-on-the-Green?"

"Sounds great, but is it possible? Don't people have trouble getting reservations there, even way in advance?"

"No problem. Professional courtesy."

Her eyebrows rose a notch, along with her estimation of him. He must be an even more highly respected nightlife figure than she knew if he commanded such recognition at one of New York's most prestigious restaurants on its busiest day.

"Should I change into something else?" she asked.

He studied her. "You might make a cute armadillo."

"Seriously."

"No, there's no dress code. Can I say good-bye to Helen? If I have a fan club of even one in this house, I'd like to preserve it."

He leaned into the kitchen. "Thank you for the tea," he told the diminutive woman.

Her heavily wrinkled pumpkinlike face became all smiles. "Hev more?"

"No! That is, I'm taking Sandy out to, uh, have tea."

Helen's grin widened. "Food also, much food for thees wan! Breeng mawny! Much dollars to feed her, beeg hawnger!"

Cale smiled uncertainly as Sandy hustled him out.

"My own public relations agency," she muttered.

"She doesn't exactly extol your virtues. And her tea tastes like turpentine, which I assume reflects her cooking ability. So she must be a good house-keeper, is that it?"

"Heavens, no. She's terrible."

Cale helped her into the red car he'd led her to. "Then why—"

"Because she and Dan have some kind of mysti-cal communication. She loves him and he trusts her. I could never work out of town or keep my strange hours if there wasn't someone I had faith in to be home with Dan. And it works out. Usually I'm only gone when he's sleeping, and I can relax knowing Helen is there. She could poison you in the kitchen, and the house would look like an abandoned crypt if I didn't clean it, but she's a warm, trustworthy per-son and she'd kill for us."

"How old is she?"

"About a hundred and six."

"No, really."

"I have no idea. Every time I ask, for Social Secu-rity forms and stuff, I get a different answer. Let the

IRS tangle with her if they want to know. They'll run off screaming."

He guided the car along the quiet suburban streets toward the Saw Mill Parkway. Greenery ran riot, the moist, hot weather having produced even more plant life than usual for early July. The steady summer hum of insects filled the car along with the sweet sun-warmed air.

"So you have two cars," Sandy said.

"Three, actually. The one I drove last night needs transmission fluid, and I didn't feel like getting up early to put it in. The other is a Toyota with front-wheel drive, which I use mostly around home in winter. Besides, there isn't enough room in it for me to watch you stretch your legs out."

Tickled by the compliment, Sandy nevertheless had the presence of mind to remember the purpose of their mission. As he turned onto Farragut, the street that ended at the parkway, she said, "Shouldn't I pick up new tires before we get into the city? I know there are places open around here on Sunday, but in town I don't—"

"You won't need new tires. Look in the back."

She turned. "There's something that looks like a scuba tank."

"It's a compressed-air pump. I can inflate your tires with it in no time."

She stared at him. "Slashed tires?"

"They're not slashed."

"But you—"

"I lied." They'd stopped for the light at the parkway entrance and he turned and looked her full in the face. "I wanted to see you again after our bust

49

up, somewhere private. What's more private than driving you back to Westchester? I knew you had a red Honda, so I just looked until I found one with a Hastings parking sticker, deflated the tires, and waited for you to leave. Plus, that gave me a built-in reason to see you today." He grinned. The sunlight on his dark hair warmed it, sending the aroma of shampoo over to her.

The driver behind beeped chidingly and Cale obeyed the green light and drove on.

A feeling of panic touched her for a moment—and then disappeared. She waited for the fury to rise, the anger at having been duped, but it didn't.

I'm *flattered,* she realized with shock. He went to all that trouble to arrange to be with me, to ensure my company.

Okay, he'd created a potentially thorny situation; but he'd solved it, gallantly and with obvious delight in her company. What more could she ask?

CHAPTER THREE

Happily Sandy watched trees and lush grass fly by, then the Hudson River with the palisades of New Jersey on its far side as they entered Manhattan. Cale turned off at the Ninety-sixth Street exit and drove through the Sunday-hushed West Side streets to Tavern-on-the-Green in Central Park.

"Hungry?" he asked as he turned the car over to an attendant and they went in. "Or is that a dumb question?"

"Idiotic. Do I sound like I'm talking through a swimming pool? Because the smell of that bacon is making me salivate to a degree that could get embarrassing."

Cale snatched a chunk of raisin pumpernickel from a passing waiter's tray. "Here, Sambu," he said. "Just to keep you from chomping on someone's arm. You should have told me before we left that you were starved. I'd have waited for you to have a snack."

"Tavern-on-the-Green sounded so good, I wanted to save my appetite. Of course, that's like saving snow in a blizzard."

The maitre d' greeted Cale warmly and showed them to a window table with a garden view. Within moments a pot of coffee and a plate of tiny, sticky honey buns were on the table, and Sandy plunged in.

There had to be more to Cale than met the eye. Owning a club—even two clubs, as he had before selling one—didn't produce the kind of income that supported three cars, nor the status that rated window tables at Tavern-on-the-Green for Sunday brunch.

"I'm impressed," she said honestly.

"Good. I'm trying to impress you. This music is an embarrassment, though," he said, cocking a critical ear. "I'll have to talk to them about it."

She hadn't even noticed there was music. Now, listening, she could pick up the muted tape. "You can hardly hear it. Does it matter?"

"Does to me. Bad music is offensive, even on a background tape."

She gathered honey bun crumbs off the plate with her fingers. "But do customers in a place like this even care what they're hearing in the background?"

He chuckled. "Don't let any of my clients hear you say that. They frequently *are* the background in a place like this."

She was silent for a minute, gazing at the eggs Sardou that had just arrived, poached eggs in a ramekin with spinach and hollandaise sauce.

"Did you say clients?" she asked.

"I manage a few singers."

That explained it. Half a dozen successful singers, his percentage from steady high-paid bookings . . . with that plus the income from his club, he must do very nicely.

"So you're sort of a combination businessman and music lover," she said, and he marveled at how readily she'd summed up the dual identity he'd carved for himself. His fail-safe career, as he often thought of it, when doubts nagged. "What's it like to be an artists' manager? Don't you ever feel strange having so much say over people's careers?"

He smiled. "I like to be the one with the reins. I guess that's why I manage."

She laughed. "I like to be the one with the reins too. I guess that's why I don't *have* a manager."

"Remind me not to go horseback riding with you. We'd have to share the saddle."

He dug into his mushroom omelet, then looked up at her and winked. Her face warmed. He was so attractive. It wasn't only that he looked good enough to model for a fitness center . . . that way he had of directing his gaze, his words, all his attention straight at her, was mesmerizing. And it wasn't as if they were alone. There were enough flowers, crystal, and beautiful people in this room to keep anyone's attention darting.

She shifted a long leg under the table and accidentally bumped him. Instead of moving, he pressed his leg closer. She nearly choked on a bite of spinach. His trouser fabric against her bare calf was sharply sensuous. She looked up from her plate and found him staring at her with a half smile. He increased the pressure on her leg for a minute and then moved away.

"More coffee?" he asked as though nothing had happened.

"Yes, thanks," she answered sweetly. "I guess that must not have been *your* leg."

He burst out laughing. "That'll teach me to be Mr. Smooth. I keep forgetting how quick you are to say what most people only think."

"Do I do that?"

"Seems like it to me."

"I never thought of it that way. I know I'm direct; I have to be in my business or I'll get squashed. Those mushrooms look delicious. Can I have one?"

"One more, you mean?"

"What?"

"You've already taken several."

"I took . . . ?"

He nodded.

"I didn't realize. I'm so embarrassed." She covered her eyes.

He pulled her hands away. "Listen, if I have you so enchanted that you don't know you're taking food off my plate, I'm not complaining. Just do it with something other than mushrooms next time, okay? Or I may have to carry a weapon. I'm *extremely* fond of mushrooms."

Chastened, she went back to her eggs. She was acting like a person under a spell. She tried to think of something to say that would put them back in the comfortable realm of small talk. No inspirations came. She buttered a croissant and ate half of it. Sunshine washed in and flooded their table. A vase of yellow rosebuds winked in a prism of color.

"So," she said, thoroughly uneasy with the silence that didn't seem to faze Cale. And then, falling back on every comic's standby, "Where are you from?"

"Boston."

She looked up. "Really?"

"Really. What's so surprising?"

"I don't hear any accent."

He shrugged. "I never had much. Probably because my folks are from New York originally. Parents are the strongest influence on your accent."

"So your family moved from New York to Boston and back again?"

"No. I'm the only one in New York. They're all still there. My father is a professor at the Boston Conservatory of Music."

Sandy's plate was empty except for a parsley sprig and a cherry tomato. She ate them, covering her mouth. If she was capable of snitching from his plate without knowing it, she wouldn't put it past herself to decorate his shirt with tomato seeds.

"What brought you here?" she asked.

"I went to Juilliard."

"That's interesting. Even though your father . . . ?"

"Uh-huh," he said, and busied himself pouring coffee.

She started to pursue the point, but he'd discovered the pot was empty and was signaling for another. Something in his distracted manner told her he'd prefer not to discuss this. Sure enough, he changed the subject himself.

"You're not mad that I deflated your tires, are you?" he asked. "It was the best I could do on short notice."

"I should be mad."

"But you're smiling."

"Then I guess I'm not mad."

Her hand was resting on the tablecloth and he held it. He leaned toward her. They were as close now as they'd been when he lifted her from the couch in her house, and his nearness caused flutters under her skin. The carved handsomeness of his face made her a little breathless. There was color in his forehead beneath the side-brushed dark hair, just enough to show he felt the pull, too, the wish to be closer still.

"Vandalism isn't my style," he said, his thumb tracing the bones in the back of her hand, "but I didn't want to leave things bad between us. I'd already made you angry twice last night. Seems like that's not hard to do." She said nothing, and he went on, "I figured my best chance of getting you alone and quiet for a while was to make you need me."

She smiled wryly. "That *is* hard to do."

"Well, I succeeded, so the crime was worth it."

"Good thing you didn't get caught."

He rubbed his brow. "I never thought of that."

"Are you serious?"

"Yes. It never occurred to me that I could have been, ah, misunderstood."

Sandy grinned. "I can just see—"

"I know, I know. Me trying to explain to a couple of cops the size of freighters that I was vandalizing your tires on a dark street at two A.M. because I wanted to get to know you better."

"Well, I should probably say how romantic you

were to take the risk, even if you didn't know you were taking it. But what I really want to say is, are you going to eat your parsley?"

He laughed and gave it to her. "Would you like dessert?"

"Is it warm in Death Valley? Yes, I'd like a large anything, as long as it's chocolate, and more coffee."

He watched while she started on a pastry the size of a snowshoe. "Do you eat like this all the time?"

"Only when I'm hungry."

"You don't have to watch calories?"

"No, thank goodness. It's never been a problem."

He shook his head in envious wonder. "If I ate that way, I'd have to buy new clothes every three months."

She eyed his designer shirt. "That would be hard even for you."

"Do I get a bit of that tower of cholesterol?" he asked, his fork poised.

"After I made guerrilla raids on your mushrooms? Of course." He cut a chunk. "Hey, not so big."

"You can always order another."

"I can?"

"Sure. If you'll eat it in a different neighborhood. All this chocolate is too tempting."

"Sorry. Console yourself with the thought that you're looking after my needs very gallantly. You know how to please a lady. I can't think why nobody's snapped you up by now."

"Just unlucky, I guess."

"It's hard to believe you've never been married or anything."

He grinned. "Lots of 'anything.'"

She felt a pang. Did he rush women this way all the time, then tire of them? She mulled on that thought while she finished her pastry. Maybe that was how he'd managed to stay unattached for thirty-nine years. Maybe she was on her way to becoming notch number 247 in the bed post. Maybe she'd better put on the brakes.

"And what about you?" he asked.

She scowled. "What *about* me?"

"Well, hello, sunshine. What just happened?"

"What do you mean?"

He shook his head wonderingly. "I remember that face from last night. Like a truck is coming at you, and you're determined to stop it with your bare hands. Two minutes ago you were smiling. Everything was great. What made you change so fast?"

She bit off the retort that rose immediately and made herself stay quiet. Had she overreacted? She rolled the conversation back to the point where he'd alluded to his love life. "Lots of 'anything.'" Well, if he wasn't bragging about a long string of affairs, she was a Burmese mountain lion.

"Maybe I don't like being the newest dancer in the harem," she said.

"The newest . . . ? Oh. I didn't mean anything like that." These fast turnarounds were hard to take, he thought. Did he have to scrutinize every sentence for insult potential before voicing it? Maybe it wasn't possible to get through a conversation without offending her.

"You know, Sandy," he said, his face serious, "you seem to jump to the harshest possible conclu-

58

sion when something doesn't hit you right." She started to interrupt but he rushed ahead. "If someone says 'It's raining,' you probably think, 'He wants me to get wet.' "

"When you said 'lots of anything,' " she replied, her eyes contemptuous, "you obviously—"

"Okay, so it was sophomoric. I'll give you that. But look at what I said it in response to. You implied there was something strange about my not having been married. That's a little irritating, but it's no big deal, My answer was a little irritating, too, but *that's* no big deal." He spread his hands. "Do you see what I'm getting at? People have exchanges like that all the time without going to war."

She looked away, but not before he saw the change in her face. The belligerent frown had gone. The strained lines that were already growing familiar had begun to dissolve into something that looked a lot like hurt.

"Sandy?" he said. She turned back to him, and now he was sure. "I think I see what's going on."

Her eyes went wary. "What?"

"You're being Sandy Shaw with me."

"Who do you want me to be? Leon Redbone?"

"I want you to be Sandy Shoresky."

That made her quiet, and he sat back, waiting. Would she hide behind another joke? Turn hostile again? Or would she listen?

But she surprised him. "Eureka," she said quietly. Her tone masked a nervous jump in her pulse rate. She wasn't sure she liked the turn this conversation was taking—and she wasn't sure she didn't. Her persona had been built carefully over the past six years, in many ways involuntarily. It was so entrenched that even she didn't always know where the performer stopped and the woman began. The idea that someone else might see the duality was frightening.

On the other hand, how many people had ever taken the trouble to look? If Cale was perceptive enough—and *interested* enough—to have seen past the shield she'd constructed, that was exciting.

A matching excitement rose in Cale as he watched her. He could almost see the conflicts playing themselves out behind her soft eyes. He hadn't realized how off-putting her instant anger was until he'd felt relief at the notion that it might not be a built-in, ineradicable feature of this otherwise fascinating woman.

She pushed a thick strand of red-gold curl behind her ear. The sun burnished it and made gilded feathers of her long pale lashes. He wanted to reach out and stroke the hair, touch the lashes . . . trace the sharp planes of her face.

"I'm right, aren't I?" he said. "You fly off the handle on purpose. You use it."

"I don't think it's . . . that calculated."

He could see how hard this was for her. "Maybe you ought to do the talking."

"Well . . ." She rubbed her temples. "I guess I just get defensive when someone doesn't seem to like me."

"Who doesn't get defensive then?"

She blinked. "What are you saying?"

"That in your case it goes further than that." He

saw ire building and jumped in. "Look! It's happening right now."

She relaxed a little. "You mean I get defensive faster than some people."

"You could say that," he said dryly. "Look, this is presumptuous as hell, but you seem to get bristly at the least thing I say that sounds . . . well, rejecting."

She nodded, surprising him again. He'd thought he'd have to lead her to that by the hand. Under the layers of who she was and wasn't, he thought, she was very brave.

"So beneath that hard-boiled facade you're—"

"Pudding."

A waiter brought more coffee, but neither of them noticed.

"Thanks for being so honest. It must be hard."

She smiled tentatively. "I do feel awfully naked."

"There's only one thing I don't understand," Cale said. "Why a woman so vulnerable becomes a comic. I know how brutal *that* rejection can be."

Sandy sighed. "I've thought about that a lot. It's all part of the same package. I don't want to know what quality I share with other comics that makes us try to win over hundreds of people every night, but that's the key. And it creates defensiveness. Hit them before they can hit you."

"So you're this defensive with everybody."

"I wouldn't say that."

He turned away to sign the check, but her answer hung between them like a live thing. Finally he asked, "What makes me so lucky?"

She'd talked herself into a corner. There was no

choice but to follow through. He rose and she did the same. It was only natural for him to touch her waist to guide her out, so he was holding her when she said, "I care about you."

He pulled her closer to his side and pressed her head to his for a brief, intense moment.

True to his words, Cale inflated the Honda's tires in minutes. Sandy waited in his air-conditioned car, enjoying the restful quiet of the brownstone-lined street, the contentment of having passed a personal milestone with Cale. It was unnerving and yet a relief to be less guarded, more herself, with him.

When he got back in, she was just finishing half a honey bun she'd saved.

"Again?" he asked incredulously.

She shrugged and began to lick her sugary fingers. He pried her hand from her lips and did it for her, putting each finger in his mouth and laving it thoroughly. The pull she'd felt off and on since last night had intensified, as she found more and more to like about this beguiling man; now, by the time he finished, she was bathed in pleasure. The motion of his lips, tongue, and teeth on her fingers sent rivulets of heat through her.

He pulled back to look at her face. Whatever he saw there encouraged him to continue, and he reached out a strong, tanned hand, gripped her chin, and brought his lips down on hers. Now the tongue that had caressed her fingers with its soft/ rough warmth was pushing at her lips, opening them, entering her mouth to do its magic there. It set tiny fires of delight that she responded to with her own tongue, meeting him, making him welcome. She sought and found the chip in his bottom tooth that had intrigued her, and felt a sharp thrill of fantasy realized.

He pulled her to him, stroking her fluffy curls, her neck, her cheek, as they explored each other's mouths. His hands were electric through her clothes, making her shiver.

She inhaled deeply; she loved his scent, the faint musk from his exertion on the steaming street. She pushed his collar aside so she could nip the corded muscle of his shoulder. He made a noise deep in his throat and held her nearer still. With moist lips she followed the sinew as it climbed his neck. Her kisses seemed to inflame him, and he moved his hands around to the sides of her breasts. His breathing quickened as his fingers met the beginning softness.

Sandy was growing breathless herself. His knowing, insistent touch created a mist of longing that threatened to overtake her. She was caught in a spiral of emotion that was carrying her inexorably deeper, and Cale right along with her, to an uncharted territory of feeling.

But it was midafternoon on a New York street, she forced herself to remember. The bolts of sweet fire Cale was sending through her body were stunning in their power, and she needed to edge back, not lose any more of her control to it. . . .

Cale was oblivious, lost in his sensations of her. Slowly but firmly she pulled away, trailing a pale hand along his cheek. He reacted like someone rising from the depths of a trance, reawakening by degrees. She watched the changing emotions in his face as he reoriented himself, part of him wanting them to become lost in each other once more.

"I actually forgot where we were," he told her. He leaned over, took her earlobe in his teeth for a second, and whispered, "Kissing you was so delicious, I forgot everything else."

The tiny delectable stab of his teeth, his breathy words in her ear, were almost too much for her. Sandy had to clench her hands to keep from reaching for him again.

"Thank you for feeding me," she said in a prim non sequitur that perhaps was neither. She had to get out of here; his nearness was dangerous, the temptation of those hands, those lips, too acute to bear.

She kissed his cheek and stepped out of the car. Then she unlocked the Honda, got in, and raced off, not even pausing long enough to turn the air conditioner on and cool her streaming face.

CHAPTER FOUR

"Thank you and good night!" Sandy said, striding off the stage to fervent applause and shouts of "More!" How intoxicating a set like that was! It made everything worthwhile—the years of club-footed performances, humiliating rejection, the subtle ridicule of emcees and more experienced comics. True, sometimes all you did was broil under stage lights, trying to get laughs, and earn only excruciating silence; but no high could match that of a roomful of people laughing with you, delighting in your observations. To isolate the nugget of absurdity in any situation, polish it, shape it so that an audience would roar their recognition; to play them so they saw each nuance just when you wanted them to—that was the essence of the art. And when it worked this well—bliss!

The door of Twinkles opened and Cale stepped in. Sandy was surrounded by performers congratulating her and he didn't see her right away. She took advantage of the moment to feast her eyes.

Ever since their brunch the previous weekend, and their time in his car afterward, she'd thought of Cale almost constantly. The sensations he'd stoked within her in those few minutes—truly, he must have bewitched her. She'd relived every touch, every proof of his feeling for her—his sounds, the raw strength of his arms as they clasped her, the way he'd seemed unable to let her go.

Now, while he searched for her, she watched the solid shoulders tug his jacket as he turned, the powerful hands as he put them in his pockets, the enticing hardness of his thighs in the charcoal suit, displayed sharply as he moved through the room, looking for her, for her. . . .

He spotted her and made his way over. The other performers watched with frank curiosity as he put his arm around her waist and kissed her cheek.

"Come with me for a minute?" he asked close to her ear. The tickle of his whisper sent hot darts along her nerve endings.

She followed him to the door and out, making a face as the fume-laden city smog blasted her.

"I hope you didn't bring me out here to treat me to a breath of fresh air," Sandy said.

He laughed. "I wanted to treat myself—to a little time with you. I've missed you. Had a busy few days. I knew you must have just come offstage when I heard all that noise through the wall."

She was thrilled. If he couldn't have seen the set, at least he heard the reaction. And even better: he assumed the laughter and applause were for her, not for some other comic!

"How about coming in—through the front door this time—and having a drink? I'd like to show you off." His sweeping glance of admiration took in flowing turtle-green slacks cinched with a gold belt, and a matching silk blouse.

The heat was already becoming oppressive—or was it also his smoldering gaze? Sandy lifted the heavy fall of tiny curls off her neck to let the faint breeze flutter her collar. Long white feather earrings framed her face, lighting it.

"I'd love to," she said, "if an onion loaf is part of the deal."

"Is there ever a time when you don't think about food?" he asked, following her into Caleb's.

"I guess I might not during a train wreck."

He led her to a quiet spot some distance from the stage. This was obviously the house table, kept open for him. All the rest were filled, and Sandy could see a waiter turning two couples away.

The room was spectacularly decorated in shades of burgundy with silver accents, the stage a raised kidney-shaped slab of lucite that highlighted the performer brilliantly. A slim and glamorous black woman in a mauve jumpsuit was singing, and Sandy watched with enjoyment as she finished her Latin-beat number with a little flamenco hop, to applause and cheers.

Cale beckoned her to the table and stood to hold a chair for her. "Rana McDonnell, Sandy Shaw," he said. "Sandy's also an entertainer."

That's the second time he's used that word instead of comic, Sandy thought. She started to make the correction, but Rana was already speaking.

"Great to meet you," she said, offering a cool, finely shaped hand.

Sandy clasped it. "What I heard of your set was terrific. I hope I'll get to hear more."

"Thanks. Spend any time with Cale and you sure

will. In fact, you'll hear more music than speech. I've never known anyone so committed."

A waiter appeared at Cale's elbow. "What would you two like to drink?" Cale asked them.

"Perrier with lime," Rana said. "My sets aren't over," she told Sandy.

"Mine are," Sandy said. "Vodka gimlet on the rocks, please."

"Same for me," Cale told the waiter, and he nodded and left.

"Are you a singer too?" Rana asked.

"No, I'm a c—"

"Sandy, didn't you want an onion loaf?" Cale interrupted.

"Oh, yes!"

He called the waiter back and ordered it. "Sandy can demolish an onion loaf faster than you can say heartburn," he told Rana.

Rana smiled at her. "I don't imagine that's your act, though. What were you saying you do?"

"Comedy. I'm a stand-up."

Rana's eyes widened. Cale was suddenly very interested in something over Sandy's shoulder, but when she turned, she couldn't see what it might be. Then Rana chuckled, the sound wry and throaty. What the heck was going on? She felt as if she'd been plopped into a play and was the only one who hadn't read her lines.

"Now I know this is a social visit," Rana said. "Consorting with the enemy, Cale! Naughty." She turned to Sandy. "He must like you a lot."

"Maybe it's me," Sandy said, "but I'm having a little trouble—"

"Rana's just being devilish," Cale told her.

"Forgive me, but I still don't—"

Rana leaned toward her. "I'm teasing Cale about his prejudices. He must be mellowing, though, if you're here. You work Twinkles?" Sandy nodded. "He complains about Twinkles all the time," Rana said confidingly.

"Rana—"

"Well, you do, Cale! For someone like Sandy, though, I can see why you'd make an exception."

"I know why Twinkles bothers him," Sandy said to Rana as if Cale weren't there, "but what's this about his prejudices?"

"If you two don't mind—"

Rana said, "Stay out of this. Woman talk. Go tune a harp." To Sandy, "His background is classical. He bucked a long family tradition to get into this kind of music. But he can justify jazz and soft rock as art, so they're okay. Forget anything punky or hard, and as for comedy—"

"Rana, will you cut it out?" Cale said exasperatedly. "Give me a chance with the lady, will you? Do I go around sabotaging your love life?"

Their drinks came, and Rana said something about women sticking together as she lifted hers, but Sandy was distracted. A glow was building that had nothing to do with the gimlet. Cale had referred to her as his "love life" in front of someone. That kind of made it official.

Dreamily she watched Cale and Rana tease each other. The club's pinkish light made his dark hair gleam. His smile, though it lacked the incandescence it held when he turned it on her, warmed his face as he chatted. She loved his face, its expressive mobility, the way his features turned wry with humor or soft with affection. Absently, as he talked to Rana, Cale caressed Sandy's arm, as if to show her she was part of whatever he did. She enjoyed the gentle pressure, the way her skin seemed to rise to his touch like cat's fur.

Rana took her drink and stood. "I promised I'd spend a while with those people at table nine. Nice to know you, Sandy. Hope we'll meet again. From the way Cale's behaving, I'm sure we will. I haven't seen a look in his eye like that since they brought in the concert grand over there."

Sandy hid her pleasure. She watched Rana's statuesque stride as she crossed the room. "What attitude. Some people just walk through life as if they owned it," she said admiringly.

"That's Rana. Nothing stops her, no matter what she wants to do. Including showing you all *my* cards."

He squeezed her arm and she saw the special smile, the one he seemed to save for her. It shimmered with promise. She smiled back, and her cheeks heated as she realized that her face must show what his did.

Their waiter brought the hot onion loaf. Even he seemed to sense the charge locking the two pairs of gray eyes, for he set the basket down gingerly, unwilling to interrupt. Reluctantly Cale broke the tie and turned to thank the man. Then his eyes found hers again and he said, "I've been thinking about you all week. I couldn't get Sunday out of my mind.

70

It was a wonderful day. Especially later . . . in the car."

Sandy wanted to reach out a finger and trace the contours of those chiseled lips. They spoke such lovely words—and did such lovely things, as he'd shown her that day and would show her again, though nowhere near soon enough.

Maybe she was self-conscious being on his turf, or perhaps the room was just too public for the depth of feeling they were exchanging, with and without words. Sandy felt compelled to distract herself, and she turned to the basket and took a few of the crunchy circles. When she looked up again, Cale's head was bent and he was wiping away tears.

"You really should try soft lenses," Sandy said sympathetically.

Cale sniffed and blinked. His eye seemed okay now.

"With the permanent ones, you never have these problems. Nothing can get under them, because they don't float. My whole life changed when they were invented."

"How?"

"Well, aside from the fact that I no longer feel as though my eye's been torpedoed if dirt gets in, I don't have to take them out—even to sleep or shower. I only remove them every two weeks for cleaning. Some people can go a couple of months."

"Will you help me if I get them?"

She sipped her drink. "You won't need help. They show you exactly what to do, give you sample products, a booklet—"

"I might need your assistance with some of the peripheral points."

Sandy reached for more onions. "Peripheral points?"

"The sleeping and showering."

"But—oh." Her hands fell from the onion basket. A weakening heat stole over her.

When he added, "You'll have to do those things with me at first to be sure I don't make any mistakes," she was already way ahead of him with her imagery, and the pictures in her head were making her tremble: lying with Cale in a big, firm bed, asleep in his muscled arms . . . sweet-smelling clouds billowing around them in the shower, slippery body to slippery body, their mouths meeting . . . his tanned nudity—there'd be a white area where his swimsuit had been. . . .

His eyes burned through hers, as though he knew exactly what was running on the screen behind them, and she had to look away. She took some onions and munched distractedly. But she could still feel his gaze on her, willing her to meet it again.

"Sandy?"

Startled, she looked to her right.

"I saw you at Twinkles tonight," the unfamiliar woman said. "You were so hysterical, my mascara ran."

"Oh, thanks," Sandy said, smiling.

"You're going to be the next Joan Rivers, no doubt in my mind. Well, bye, Sandy. Bye, Mr. Shaw."

Sandy laughed. "Sorry about that," she told Cale, reaching for her drink. When he didn't answer, she glanced up. He was draining his glass and looked ready to take a bite out of it.

"I don't know if you're aware of this," Sandy said, "but the expression on your face would paralyze a scorpion."

He simply glared.

"Oh, don't tell me you're miffed because someone called you Mr. Shaw? Come on, Cale, you're a professional. That should roll right off." He still wasn't smiling. "Be happy for me, will you? She called me Sandy. I feel great when that happens. It means I'm going over, that they're keying in to me as a person. That each one feels like I'm talking right to them."

He was trying to control his hostility. He'd been able to earlier, when Rana was teasing, but now the whole business was getting away from him.

"Forgive me," he said, "but I don't buy that. I know comics like to think they can manipulate an audience, play it like an instrument, but I figured you'd be above that."

"Above it?" Something chilly was gathering in her chest. "Wait a minute. This is a red herring. You were mad even before I said anything about audiences."

He was silent.

"It's the whole idea of what I do that's got you, isn't it? You keep referring to me as an entertainer. That's like calling Superman someone who flies. You were ready to start World War Three to keep me from answering when Rana asked me what I did. Some nice woman compliments me and you look murderous. Good heavens, you should see your face when you walk into Twinkles—like there's a smell your delicate nasal passages can't tolerate. Rana brought it up, and you shushed her. What *is* it with you and comedy, anyway?"

"I just don't care for it, that's all. It's not my thing."

"It's not your thing?" Sandy screeched, so incensed that she forgot she was in his club, surrounded by his associates and a full house of paying customers. The sound system was loud, but only a sonic boom could have drowned her out entirely.

"You can dispose of my entire career with one mean little statement? Do you have any idea how long it takes to become even passable at this, compared with learning to sing? At least I'm a functioning artist. I don't just make a lot of money directing other people's talent!"

"At least I make a lot of money!" he thundered back at her. "At least I have a civilized profession, not a pseudoartistic nonjob!"

She jumped up. It was all she could do not to heave her drink in his face. Let him pry his contact lenses off her ice cubes.

"This pseudoartist is leaving," she spat. "You can keep your civilized tail out of Twinkles and out of my life!"

Without looking back she stalked to the door and out.

"Who?" Sandy mumbled groggily from beneath her comforter, her mouth feeling as though she'd bitten into a piece of upholstered furniture.

"Foller," Helen repeated.

Sandy's eyes snapped open. "He's here?" she shouted, throwing off the bedclothes.

"No, no. Phone," Helen said, pantomiming a receiver at her ear. "I tell him call back."

"No!" she yelled as Helen started to leave. "I'll talk to him. What time is it?"

"Nine-tawty."

She closed her eyes and moaned. "I need a few minutes. Ask him to hold on, will you, Helen?"

She stumbled into the bathroom, tied her hair back, splashed her face. She hadn't heard from Cale since their fight Saturday night. She'd thought of him often yesterday, wondering whether he'd call, whether she even wanted to talk to him. One thing was sure: her defensiveness didn't deserve all the blame for her fury this time. She still trembled with anger when she thought of the rotten things he'd said.

She dried off, rubbing her eyes, which could now rest about half open without conscious effort. Five hours of sleep wasn't enough for a bat.

She was keeping Cale waiting, but that was tough. "I'm worth waiting for," she told the pale redhead in the mirror.

"Hah?" Helen called from just outside, and Sandy jumped.

"Nothing." Helen said something unintelligible, and Sandy opened the door. "What?"

"Foller say come talk. He miss you." Helen grinned.

"That's very nice. Is missing me his thing? Never mind," she said hastily as Helen's mouth began to form a question.

She picked up the phone in the kitchen. "Hello, Cale."

"It's good to hear your voice," he said, his own rough, throaty, as if he'd just gotten up. "I guess I woke you."

"That's right."

"Sorry. I wanted to catch you—"

"Well, you caught me. My ear, at least."

He sighed. Her words were brittle, chilled. He'd expected her to be mad, and she sure as a hornet was. "Then I guess it's up to me to say the right things into it."

"I don't know if I'm interested in hearing whatever you think the 'right things' are."

"That's too bad, because I want you to. In person. That's the only way. If you have any plans for the day, I'd like you to change them. You're not working tonight, are you?"

"No," she said, wondering what he'd suggest, her heart already fluttering in spite of herself. "Twinkles has auditions tonight and everyplace else is pretty dead. I usually don't work Mondays and Tuesdays."

"Will you spend the day with me?"

She hesitated. Helen handed her a cup of coffee and left the kitchen. "I'm very angry at you."

"That makes two of us. I was a creep. I'm sorry. I care for you so much, and I seem to be showing you everything but."

Her pulse grew faster. He cared for her! He'd used the word *much!*

"I just hope I haven't driven you away for good. I really want to be with you, Sandy."

He really wanted to be with her! She took a sip of

coffee to calm herself, made a prune face, dumped the rest down the sink.

"Sandy?"

"Yes, sorry," she said. "I had a mouthful of Helen's janitor-in-a-coffee-cup."

"That's it! Will you see me if I promise to feed you well?"

"You don't have to bribe me, Cale."

"I don't?"

"Of course not. But since you mentioned it, what kind of food did you have in mind?"

He laughed. "What do you usually have for breakfast?"

"Just something light. Pot roast, veal parmigiana—"

"How does barbecued spare ribs sound?"

"Great."

"Can you be here in a half hour?"

She paused, muddled. "Be where?"

"At my place. In Tarrytown."

"You're going to cook for me?" It was only one of at least a dozen questions that had suddenly popped up.

"It's the least I can do, don't you think?"

"Yes. I do think." Her mind was racing, whirling around one thought now: It's a little less public than Seventy-first street. "But give me an hour."

"Okay. It's fourteen Valley Road, the condos overlooking the river. And hurry. I'm hungry. *Really* hungry."

And not just for spare ribs, I'll bet, she thought with a shiver of anticipation as she hung up.

She climbed the steps to his door at ten forty-five and paused before ringing the bell to enjoy the view. The oppressive July humidity had taken a day off. Sun sparked the wide Hudson below, and the sky was a sweep of blue with puffs of cloud.

"It looks even prettier from my terrace," Cale said behind her, and she turned. He wore old soft jeans and a T-shirt. His tan was luminous, making the silver-gray eyes gleam like opals, and she remembered thinking disdainfully when they met that he probably liked the Hamptons. Little did she know that he'd done his sunning just ten minutes north of where she lived.

"Let me introduce you," he said, leading her inside. Before she had time to wonder who she was going to meet, she found herself being stared at by a Siberian husky and a long-haired tan-and-white cat.

"This is Isabel," he said, stroking the dog's huge head, "and that's Milt."

Sandy knelt and tentatively petted one with each hand. They were a bit distant, but willing to give her a chance.

"They're lovely," she said. Cale joined her and the animals on the floor. His bare arm brushed hers. The intimate appeal of his soap-and-toothpaste, just-got-up smell caused her to sink to a sitting position. Milt promptly crawled into her lap and curled up. Isabel whined.

"She's jealous," Cale said, laughing. He kissed the dog's nose. "She wishes she wasn't too big to sit on laps. Oh, hey, you haven't had your transfusion. Come with me."

Sandy carefully dislodged the cat and followed

Cale through the airy living room into the kitchen. It was cream and green, with a large butcher-block table in the work area that looked as though he actually used it to cut things on. Sliding glass doors opened onto the terrace. The view created an effect of continuous space. Imagine being able to look at the river while you slice string beans, she thought.

He pressed a coffee mug into her hands and she sipped.

"You like it?"

"It's wonderful. Do you do windows?"

He grinned. "Wait'll you taste the rest. Ribs, salad, and garlic bread. Think that's enough breakfast for you?"

She drank more coffee. Its bittersweet bite was revivifying. "You seem to be trying to make up for the things you said Saturday."

He chuckled ruefully. "That's my Sandy—coming right out with it. Yes, I am trying to. I'm sorry for insulting you. I realize I don't take your work seriously enough, but I have to change that, since I take *you* seriously. Though probably not quite as seriously as you take yourself. You like to call the shots most of the time, don't you?"

"Where did you get that idea?"

"From about two thirds of the things you say and do."

She nodded.

"So you agree it's a fault."

"Yes. One we share."

He grinned. "Point for the lady with the red eyes. Is the coffee helping at all?"

"Uh-huh." She held out her cup for more. "But

79

as long as we're hanging our quirks out to dry . . . why are you so prickly about what I do? It isn't just a matter of not taking my work seriously, is it?"

He turned to the sink and rinsed out a pan. He was at it so long, Sandy began to wonder whether he'd answer.

"Maybe not," he said at last.

"So if—"

"It's a beautiful day," he said, putting the pan away. "We have better things to talk about than our work."

"Our work," she mused, watching him, her analytical mind chugging away. "Maybe I'm not the only one whose profession you have trouble taking seriously. Oh! Bull's-eye, huh?" she said as he winced. "These pieces must fit together. You started out in classical music . . . you're some kind of maverick in the family, is that it?"

"Something like that. There's a lot more to it—"

"There generally is."

"—but I won't bore you. You don't want to hear the ins and outs of the music business."

"I like hearing about you, though," Sandy said.

A smile started to push up the corners of his mouth. It spread across his tanned face, lighting it. He grabbed her in a bear hug, kissed her nose, and released her. "That's all we need. We'll be fine. Here, toss the salad while I put the ribs on. Not with the spoon, with your *paws*. . . ."

Later they sat on the private, enclosed terrace with more coffee, watching the river and the palisades beyond.

80

"What's for dessert?" Sandy asked dreamily.

He leaned across her in the glider and licked her lower lip.

"Isn't that tastier than ice cream?" he asked near her ear.

"Do I have to decide?" she whispered back, but her insides were jelly, belying her flip answer. The slick softness of his tongue on her lip, the freshly laundered smell of his denims and T-shirt, were devastating.

"Maybe you'd rather have a sundae than"—he kissed her gently and sweetly, the tip of his tongue darting out to tease her lips open for just an instant —"this."

He pulled back and looked at her. Holding his gaze, Sandy licked her mouth, as though considering which she'd prefer.

"Well?" he asked.

She couldn't continue this pretense of indifference any longer. She had to have more of that beautiful mouth, those arms she already knew could be so forceful and yet so easy, that body she'd watched with longing. Her eyes never leaving his, she slowly reached out and wrapped her arms around his shoulders.

"Sandy," he whispered, and his hands came up behind her back to tangle in her hair as they kissed. Hungry mouth pressed to hungry mouth, dark lashes brushing pale, they spoke their feelings with their tongues and lips for long moments in the sweet July afternoon.

After a while Sandy pulled away and rested her head in the crook of Cale's shoulder as he sat back.

She wanted only to stay like this for now, to enjoy his nearness, the languid day, the vista of water, trees, and sky all at once. She wanted to stretch their time together, make it last, keep aware of every detail.

Cale hugged her tighter, as though he knew what she was thinking and felt the same. She sighed with happiness and absently began to rub his upper torso, the sensitive pads of her fingertips feeling the play of tough muscle beneath his shirt.

"Make three wishes," he said.

She giggled and snuggled deeper against him. "It's lovely here," she said, "and the glider is neat. Why doesn't it creak? I remember them from when I was a kid. Everybody with a big porch had one. But they made so much noise you could hear a symphony of metal every night in the neighborhood."

"I oiled it. Just before you got here, as a matter of fact." He shifted around to look directly at her. "I wanted it to be quiet for us."

Her face reflected surprise, then touched pleasure, then desire as the meaning of his words penetrated. He must have planned that they'd . . . right here on the . . .

He pushed her long curls back, away from her face. His fingers stroked the smooth skin of her cheeks and he kissed her eyelids, flicking his tongue out to touch the lashes, and moved down to trail his lips along her jawline and nip her plump pink earlobes.

Sandy couldn't stop thinking about what he'd said. "I wanted it to be quiet for us." She felt as if she'd been there watching him oil the metal slides, testing it by shaking the glider with his hand, inserting more oil. In her mind's eye she saw him give it the final test, sitting down, maybe lying on it . . . thinking of her, perhaps fantasizing her beneath him on the cushion. . . .

Dizzy with yearning, she reached for him, arching to fit herself against his body. He clasped her tightly to his chest and then slipped his hands under her blouse. He caressed her back, learning the knots of her spine, and discovered with a quick sweep of his fingers that her bra hooked in front. He moved around and snapped it gently open with one hand.

"Cale, mmm," she said as his palms pressed the satiny roundness and his fingers trailed licks of flame across her nipples and along the velvet insides of her upper arms. Small quakes of passion were beginning all through her body, and her hands itched to explore him as well, to know the hairy hardness of his muscular flesh, its warmth . . . to touch and kiss, express her feeling for him with her hands and mouth, as he was doing with her.

She reached for his shirt at the same instant as Cale began to undo her blouse. When he realized what she'd started, he dropped his hands. With his eyes he urged her to continue, his gaze heavy with caring, with wanting. She pushed the shirt up and he shifted to help her pull it over his head; but as soon as she saw the smooth, brown torso she'd exposed, she had to bend and kiss it, feel its textures with her mouth and rub her cheek against it. His hands rested lightly on her shoulders, and she could almost feel electricity flowing from them into her, the barest crackle of energy that told her he was holding himself back, delighting in her caresses, urging her to love him in whatever way her instincts guided her.

Now she wanted the rest of his upper body bared, and she pulled his shirt off, watching the flex of his arm muscles, admiring his chest with its black hair, the shoulders that looked even more enormous without clothes. He sat still, his eyes closed in pleasure while she kissed and nuzzled his flesh, taking tiny love bites that made him groan with longing.

Finally he eased her back and unbuttoned her blouse, his fingers trembling slightly, but deft and sure. He pushed the blouse and her lacy open bra off her shoulders and pulled her to him, his hands more urgent on her back now, pressing her breasts against the soft hair of his chest.

"Ahhh!" Sandy said, the sound escaping her throat of its own volition. Her ecstasy was so profound that every touch, every new feeling, was another plateau of sensory thrill. Cale was kissing her shoulders, nipping, making her shiver. He bent his head to know her breasts with his mouth, his tongue leaving moist ribbons of heat that set her skin ablaze.

Just when she was wondering if she might actually faint with joy, he pulled away from her and stood. Briefly she missed his arms, his lips; but then she realized what he was doing and she sat up in the glider to watch, entranced, while he unzipped his jeans and took them off. When he removed his shorts and straightened, she could only draw in a thrilled breath at his beauty. She could have watched him for hours. Hoping he'd wait before joining her on the glider again, Sandy let her passion make her bold as her eyes drank in the wonderful chest and shoulders, the solid pelvis that was, as she'd imagined, sunless white, in exciting contrast to the bronze of the rest of him . . . the path of black hair leading downward from his flat stomach . . . the treelike thighs she'd yearned to touch.

She looked up to begin a return trip, but Cale pulled her to her feet. Gray eyes met their twins for a smoldering moment. Then he kissed her lips, quickly, hungrily . . . and, without shifting his gaze from hers, opened her navy cotton trousers and let them drop. Her eyes told him she wanted this, ached for them to love each other, just as he desired it. And the message of love she saw in his warmed her all the way through and told her that whatever delights they'd known together, even greater joy was yet to come.

He kissed her mouth again, hooking his thumbs in her panties and pushing them down far enough so that he could clasp her buttocks and hold her to him—so that their bodies could meet totally, smooth breasts against sinewy chest, long legs against hard, hairy ones, satiny feminine midsection against male heat.

They stood that way for long, thrilling moments, whispering love sounds, hands stroking each other ravenously, mouths nibbling, wanting. At last, with what seemed a great effort, he moved away. He knelt and pulled her panties all the way off, paused to rest his cheek against her, causing her to cry out. Then, because they could both wait no longer, he eased her back down on the glider and, again with his eyes locked on hers, made them one, blinking in ecstasy at the instant of union.

Sandy pulled him to her with her hands, her legs. She was beyond control, conscious of nothing but the crazed joy of the moment, her love for this man and his for her as they soared together toward the summit of all feeling. His hands slid underneath her and kneaded, caressed, bespeaking his mounting passion.

"Cale!" she shouted, way past caring whether her voice carried beyond the private terrace to the grounds below. And then they were being borne on a stream of flame, propelled farther and farther along, reaching, grasping, now hitting the crest, their wordless sounds heralding their love in the quiet afternoon. They held each other tightly as their rapture peaked and then slid slowly, easily down into a loving quietude.

"I told you and now I've shown you," Cale said huskily, his weight a delicious burden on her slender body. "I take you *very* seriously."

CHAPTER FIVE

The Lincoln inched along the Long Island Express-way. Bumper to highly polished bumper, cars stretched ahead in an endless heat-hazed ribbon.

"Who would have thought the highway would crowd up so early?" Cale asked.

"Me," Sandy said. "I wanted to leave at noon, remember?"

He nodded. "I guess I should have listened."

"I guess. Of course, then we wouldn't have had lunch."

"And I would have had to listen to your stomach growl all the way to Southampton."

"Not all the way. It doesn't start till one or so."

"Why is the traffic so heavy? It's not even four."

Sandy shrugged. "I think it's part of the status game. The earlier you can take off from work for the weekend, the more powerful you are. You know," she said, shifting on the seat to face him, "when I first met you, I thought you were part of the Hamptons crowd."

His eyes widened and then he burst into laughter. "Me? Why?"

"You looked so well cared for—and the tan,

mostly. That's a world-class tan. Little did I know you got it practically on my doorstep."

"And that's where I'll keep getting it, if this is what you have to go through to spend a weekend on Long Island. Then they do this again on Sunday only in reverse, right? Good thing we're coming back tonight."

"We don't have to if we're too tired, though. The room is mine for the night if I want it."

"Up to you," Cale said. "If you're tired after the second show, we'll stay over. There won't be any traffic tomorrow."

His hand was resting on the seat between them, and Sandy pressed it. "I'm glad you're with me."

"So'm I. I'd follow you anywhere." He grinned. "Except Long Island again. The Everglades, maybe, but—"

"The Everglades can't be any harder for you than all the time you've spent in Twinkles the last month." She squeezed his hand again. "You're a good sport."

"Nope. I'm a lousy sport who happens to be in love."

It was nearly six by the time they got to the Kenilworth Inn. A wilted Cale looked hungrily at the pool as they passed it on their way to the lobby, but Sandy barely noticed. She was already gearing up for the dinner show, checking out the guests, taking a good look at the nightclub.

While she showered, Cale ordered dinner from room service. She was just stepping out in panties and bra, toweling her hair, when there was a knock.

Cale hustled her back into the bathroom, closed the door, and let the waiter in.

"All clear," he called when their dinner was set up. She came out. "Don't you have a peignoir?" he asked.

Sandy giggled. "Sure. It's right over there, next to your spats."

"You know what I mean. Something you can put on until you're ready to get dressed."

"No. I didn't think to bring anything. I'm not used to having company. Will I bother you, eating like this?" she asked, pausing by the chair he'd pulled out.

Cale pushed back her damp, fragrant hair, and kissed her neck. "It's a little distracting."

"Sorry. I'll just throw on my jeans."

"No, don't." He sat down. "I've never had dinner with a woman in her underwear before. This should be interesting."

Sandy smiled as she cut into her steak. "I should have brought a robe. It didn't occur to me. I'm so used to this whole routine on out-of-town jobs— order room service, get in the shower, come out, and dinner's ready. I just tell them on the phone to open the door." He nodded with amusement. "Well, I *did* promise to show you all aspects of a gig if you came with me. It can't be much different for me than for a singer, though. Besides, you've heard my routine so often, I have to do *something* to keep you from getting bored."

"Well, you're succeeding." They ate in silence for a few minutes. "No. I take it back."

She looked up. "You're bored?"

"Stiff."

She swallowed.

"Did you think I meant that?"

She nodded.

He laughed softly and reached across the table to stroke her drying curls. "I'm kidding, of course. I wondered how far you'd go to keep me entertained. Maybe I could have had you standing on your hands and reciting Chaucer while pouring coffee with your toes."

"Maybe. But no fair taking advantage of me in this condition."

"Undressed, you mean?"

"No. Uptight."

"You're nervous?"

"Sure."

He shook his head. "You don't act it."

"I always am when I do something other than a showcase performance in town. I'm edgy then, too, naturally, but not like this." And you're here, and I'm glad, and I want to be good. . . .

"I wouldn't have known, that's all. You seem so composed."

"Well, enjoy it, because I'll be a lot less composed an hour from now. If you think I'm scatty before I go on at Twinkles, wait'll you see this."

And indeed, by eight, Sandy could have been a different person. Watching her from the corner of his eye as he put on a dress shirt and tie, Cale saw her moving her lips, shaking her head, and gesturing while she did her face and hair. She'd pause with the shadow wand poised over a gilded eyelid to bare her teeth in a wolfish grin. One earring went on, a cascade of blue beads to match her bright dress, and then she did two kick-turns before putting on the other.

His lips twitched in amusement, but he kept quiet. What would you have thought, he asked himself, if two months ago someone had said you'd be spending the first Friday night in August in a hotel room with a lovely woman behaving like a Bellevue escapee?

Then again, he couldn't remember when he'd had so much fun. Sandy wasn't only witty onstage, she made him laugh all the time and brought out the best of his sense of humor. He found himself saying the funniest things when he was with her.

The next time he looked up, she was doing her relaxation routine, loosening her limbs and breathing deeply. He'd seen that enough times in the city to know she was about ready to go on.

She straightened and gave herself a final once-over in the mirror.

"You look beautiful," Cale said, coming up behind her. Her hair shone in the overhead light; tight circlets tumbled over her forehead and around her shoulders. The dress was made for motion, swirling as she moved, and the electric blue, rather than overpowering her gray eyes, deepened them to bottomless glowing pools.

She smiled at him. He kissed her temple gently, feeling the tickle of soft hair, and they went downstairs.

Her cheeks glowing, Sandy made her way through the crowded lobby with Cale. Encores after both shows! People kept stopping her to compliment and congratulate. The post-performance high that was part thrill, part relief, had her shaky, and she clung tightly to Cale's hand.

"I don't want to stay," she said as they went upstairs. "I'm too wired to sleep now anyway, and I'd just as soon go back if you don't mind driving."

"Nope." He squeezed her shoulders. "Let's change and we'll be on the way."

She packed away the dress and pulled on her comfy jeans. Still giddy, she moved as if in a daze, doing things automatically—and carelessly. She was just about to put hair spray under her arms when she caught herself.

"Of course, a lot of that is because you're here," she said.

"What?"

Sandy looked up. "Oh. Sorry. I finished a thought out loud. I was thinking that I'm always ditzy after a show that goes this well, but I . . ." She faltered, suddenly shy. "I'm even higher tonight because I wanted—I wanted you to see me kill, your first time out of town with me."

"I've told you fifty times—they loved you."

Sandy grinned. "I knew you'd start to appreciate comedy if you gave yourself a chance. You're really coming to like it, aren't you?"

The hopeful note escaped neither of them.

"Watching you work is a pleasure," he answered as honestly as he could. "Come on, finish packing up and let's see if there's anyplace still open where a guy can buy a star a hot fudge sundae."

An hour later they were on their way back to

Westchester. Alone with Cale in the dark, the night-warm sea-scented breeze blowing her curls back, Sandy felt relaxed and happy. Her love had grown and was returned. Thanks to patience and sensitivity on both their parts—and a bitten lip, more than once—they were building a harmony that was precious. She was learning not to lose her temper at the drop of a wisecrack. She was proud of the times she sat on her hands when her impulse was to take charge. Being in love seemed to make her want to change, to bring her closer to Cale.

When she let herself think about it, though, she was still uneasy about Cale's attitude toward comedy. She'd been trying to lead him carefully into her world. If she could get him to see the craft for all it was, appreciate her satisfaction in it, then, she hoped, his artistic judgment would win out over whatever his prejudice was.

He'd gone along willingly as she showed and instructed, teaching him about timing, attitude, delivery, working an audience, bending her material to its rhythm. She'd explained the high-wire excitement of ad-libbing, staying away from material, seeing how long you could hold them on your wits alone. She'd sat with him as they watched other comics navigate the ebb and flow of the room, predicting when they'd save a foundering set or lose it.

And now, finally, the triumph of showing him two killer shows to a tough room, all high-tech jaded weekenders in designer everything . . . now he really knew what she could do. He'd seen comedy—*her* comedy—at its best. Maybe tonight would clinch things. Soon there might be no barriers between them at all.

She slid lower in the soft seat. Cale reached out and began to stroke her thigh, his hand warm and seductive on the denim.

"I know you're exhausted—I'm taking you home to sleep. But how about staying over tomorrow?" he asked.

"Mmm," she said. She envisioned how the night would go. Two Twinkles sets, maybe some time with Cale at his club in between, then home to Tarrytown and a heavenly night in his big bed. Isabel and Milt for company . . . the refreshing breeze off the Hudson . . .

His hand inched higher and she covered it with hers. "You've convinced me," she said.

He retreated to less tantalizing territory. "I'll count on it, then."

Twinkles was packed Saturday night. It was the kind of smoky, querulous, unpredictable crowd that could turn great or terrible on a dime. Sandy coasted through her first set, putting down a couple of hecklers before they could get disruptive, earning moderate laughs and respectful applause.

"On this sort of night I'm happy if I just don't end up in the soup," she told Cale between shows at his club. "There's a full moon, a restless edge you can feel. . . ."

He raised skeptical brows.

"Really. You know I'm not superstitious. The moon does have an effect. Ask any psychologist. Or bartender. Crazy people get crazier, and even normal people get strange. It does something to crowd dynamics." She could see a tolerant look begin to take shape on his face, and she abandoned the topic. "Anyway, you'll come in for my last set? Before we . . . leave?"

There was a smoldering moment of quiet as their eyes met and they both envisioned the hours to come. Last night had left them with a yearning for each other that wasn't to be satisfied then. Sandy felt now that she could drown in those translucent eyes, sink beneath them into the floating delight that was Cale's lovemaking. She knew the hard beauty that lay beneath the impeccable clothes, the enchantment to be found in his steellike arms, the powerful body when it enveloped hers. She longed to reach out and run her hand over the carved hills and valleys of his face, touch the faint bristle along his jawline. If they hadn't been in his club, surrounded by customers and employees—many unable not to watch the couple whose link held such a potent electricity that it could have been a chain of sparks . . . but they were, and limits prevailed. Only with their eyes could they speak the volumes their minds and bodies felt.

There was a second when Cale, unwilling to have his yen for her wholly denied, gripped her small neck with his hand. Sandy felt pressure, his silent message that he wanted nothing more at this instant than to press harder, much harder . . . hard enough to bring her face to his, her lips to where he could cover them, enter, love her with his mouth. But then, as if afraid of what his hands might do, unbidden, were he to tempt himself further, he released her and sat back in his chair.

"I'll be there," he said.

And he was, slipping into a seat at the house table Virgil kept available only under the direst pressure. Knowing he'd give it up instantly rather than turn away a paying customer, Sandy had made a point of telling him Cale was coming. She'd even put a Reserved sign on it herself, so he couldn't "forget."

He arrived just as Sandy was being introduced. She walked on, letting her face radiate her authority, her aura take over the stage. She removed the mike from the stand slowly, buying time. She was trying to gauge her reception by the faces at the few tables she could see with the stage lights in her eyes. The second-show crowd was like the first: they'd give her a chance, a brief one. If she blew it, she'd have a zoo on her hands in nothing flat.

"Hi, I'm Sandy. Enjoying the show?" she began, and was horrified to hear the mike cut out after four words.

Holding the cord in tight to its connection, hoping that would do the trick, she peered at the mike as if searching for a label. "Mattel," she muttered. There was a small but encouraging burst of laughter. "Hope they don't make pacemakers," she added, and was off and running.

About five minutes in she was rolling smoothly, blessing the mike foul-up that had gotten her off to a friendly start by gaining the crowd's sympathy. One of her punchlines died. She tapped the mike. The save worked. She was about to slide into her next piece when a man to her left said, "We heard you."

She glared, but went on as if he hadn't spoken. "I was born in New Jersey—the only place where you have to brush your teeth *after* drinking a glass of water. Anyone here from my home state?" Some hands went up. She heard the man who had interrupted start to say something, and she steamrolled over him. "Ask the waiter for your special welcome cocktail. The Trenton Colada. It's made with rum, pineapple juice, and toxic chemical waste." The hearty laugh started to ebb, and she drew in a breath to continue.

"Get the hook," her heckler called. She felt the audience getting restive, squirmy. It was time.

She turned toward the man. "Do you want to step outside and say that? Good," she said, giving him no chance to answer. "You go ahead, and I'll stay here and do what I'm doing."

There was a sharp roar of relieved laughter. Sandy could see the man trying to reply, but he was drowned out. She turned away from him, as if dusting off her hands after a scuffle, and continued with her material. "Anyone here from California? Are you mellow? Is it contagious? Because—"

"I'm from Jersey," the heckler said belligerently.

Sandy felt a stab of exhilaration. The man wasn't going to give up. His rudeness had reached the point where the audience would accept whatever she did to squelch him. How fabulous that Cale was here! He'd seen her heckled before, but never with such persistence. Manipulating a situation like this for maximum laugh power was her strength. She loved the thrill of its unpredictability.

She turned her full attention to the man. "What's your name?" she asked.

"*My* name?"

"Well, I already know mine." Laughter.

"Fred Flintstone," he said, grinning.

The audience was silent except for a few groans.

"They loved that, Fred," she said. "See how easy this is? That's why I'm up here with a mike, and you're down there paying four-fifty a drink for Scotch that's made in Taiwan. By the way, was the person who gave you that shirt mad at you?"

As the laughs rolled over her, she glanced quickly toward Cale, eager to see his face. But he was hidden by the lights.

The man started to speak. "Fred," she interrupted, "when you go to the movies, do you talk to the screen?"

It was an old line but they loved it, and it shut him up. She finished her set in peace, the audience totally with her. The heckler tried to rally once, and she zapped him with casual finesse.

She came offstage amid hard applause, scanning the room for Cale. He'd left the table; he wasn't at the bar either. She spotted him by the door. He motioned for her to come outside with him.

She went, still tingling with the excitement of her performance. The humid air that had annoyed her earlier and made her clothes stick, now was a soft kiss on her flushed face.

"Was all that really necessary?" Cale asked. It took a moment for the question to penetrate, and for Sandy to realize he wasn't smiling.

She stared. "Was what necessary?"

"That . . . verbal bullfight." He waved a hand as though to dispel an unwelcome odor. "You shouldn't lower yourself."

"I didn't! I handled him brilliantly!"

He snorted. "All you did was give some lowlife a lot of attention, when the attention should be focused on *you.*"

Disappointment and anger welled in her. She fought them down. He didn't understand, that was all. He was used to musicians, not comics. She could clear up this misconception without losing her cool if she'd just keep that in mind.

"Let me explain what I was doing. This guy made a couple of rude interruptions—"

"Like hell! He was a sleaze. You shouldn't have—"

"I was simply—"

"You're not there to—"

"Are you doing your impression of him?" she yelled in frustration. Horns blared in a traffic jam that snarled the avenue, but she outshouted them. Passersby glanced over. "You're making it harder for me to talk than he did!"

"Don't compare me to some lunatic who howls at midnight. I'm only trying to show you—"

"Oh, please," Sandy said. "Is this going to be You'll-hate-this-but-it's-for-your-own-good? Interpersonal relations cliché number forty-one-b? Even my mother stopped humming that one years ago."

Cale looked highly offended. "If you're determined to reduce everything I say to a pollyanna package that shows how clever you are, then forget it."

"But I am clever, Cale! I survive on my wits up there. That's what I was trying to explain, but you wouldn't give me a chance. You've never performed. You don't know how it is on the other side of those lights."

He took her arm. This was getting too public. They'd have their own audience out here in a second. "Let's get on the road," he said. "My place can close without me."

They'd come into the city together in Cale's car, Sandy looking forward to the evening and, especially, its aftermath. Now she felt let down. Everything had been great until a few minutes ago. She didn't understand what was happening.

Cale's head was also spinning with disjointed thoughts as they walked along Seventy-third to the Lincoln. He'd felt a strange mix of pride and revulsion, watching her handle that creep. He'd wanted to grab the guy, drag him to the door, and heave him out. But Sandy had been so clearly in her element, every inch the professional.

He, too, had looked forward to now—heading back toward Tarrytown with Sandy at his side, anticipating her exciting warmth, enjoying how her special smell filled the car. But a wall was there now, something invisible but thick between them.

They got into the car. "I didn't mean to rush at you like that," he said, and felt the wall shrink some.

Sandy relaxed a little at the words. Her post-set glow had been doused by Cale's reaction. She tried to get it back. She'd earned it; it was hers.

Cale seemed more at ease now. She decided to try

100

again to explain. This time she'd be sure and get the nuances across. Maybe it hadn't been fair to expect him to understand before. He was a music person, after all. And why, really, should any non-comic— much less someone used to polite attention during a performance—see what she found so marvelous about having her set interrupted with crass comments?

They were getting onto the West Side Highway. The Hudson rippled darkly to their left. She groped for a way to begin without sounding as though she wanted to argue again. But before she could speak, he said, "You know, I've seen other comics come down on hecklers like that, bang-bang-bang. I always thought they were insensitive jerks who liked to make fools of people. I never figured I'd see you carrying on any longer than you had to if someone interrupted. I still don't understand why you didn't shut the guy up right away, or have Virgil do it."

This was her opportunity. "Good question," she said, and knew she sounded patronizing when she saw a muscle tense in his cheek. "Okay, lousy question." The save didn't work. He turned to scowl at her. "Why don't we forget I said those two things, and I'll just answer it?"

He nodded briefly.

"You can't squash a heckler too soon, or the audience thinks you're a bully. You have to give him enough rope so that they get antsy wondering if you'll do anything about it. You build the tension just so—until there's no chance they'll sympathize with him—and then, zap. As long as he asks for it, you can do anything."

"Why let it go on, though? Why let your performance be interrupted? Instead of saying sarcastic things that put him on the defensive, you should just let him know he can't do that."

Sandy felt impatience rising. She took a deep breath and let it out slowly. "You have to let him go on because . . . well, you may have trouble with this, but the reason is that it makes your act better."

She saw disgust in his face. It was getting harder to tamp down her feelings. "Correct me if I'm wrong," she said, her tone leaving no doubt as to the reception he'd get if he tried, "but I can't help wondering if you've made up your mind on this. I have the vaguest suspicion that nothing I say will change your opinion."

He was silent. He could have made a biting comeback, but he didn't. She decided to give it one more try.

"An audience knows the difference between material and ad-libbing. When some idiot at a table gives you a hard time, and you handle him humorously, it's twice as funny as the rest of the act—because *they know you're making it up.* You weren't far off when you called it a bullfight. Some comics get so rattled by hecklers, their acts are ruined. It happens to be a strength of mine—a valuable one. The crowd knows they're watching a duel, and they love it. They know I have to kill or be killed."

There was quiet while Sandy thought he might be mulling over what she'd said, trying to understand.

"I just wish you didn't *like* it so much!" he said finally. His words were a small explosion.

Sandy turned to him in shock. "What kind of crazy thing is that to say?"

"It's not crazy! You like getting up there and throwing your weight around. Zinging one-liners at some poor slob who can't spell the name of his street."

"Oh, now he's a poor slob? What happened to the sleazeball lowlife who rudely interrupted my act? Make up your mind, Cale. Am I a victim or the Marquis de Sade?"

He waved her question away. "That isn't the point. You're a comedic artist. Sparring with a customer in a dingy nightclub for peanuts doesn't dignify your talent or make good use of it. If you didn't have such a need to pull the strings, call the shots, this stuff wouldn't appeal to you."

"I'm not sure what you mean." I'm not sure I want to, she thought. "It sounds like you're saying my entiré career is a waste, but of course, I must be mistaken."

"You are," he said, refusing her bait. "I'm saying you have a strong instinct for taking control. But I'd like to see you use it differently. You should turn it inward, not spend it on some fool. *That's* the waste."

"Turn it inward?"

"Yes. Use it to enhance your art by building more *self*-discipline. The way musicians and actors do."

Sandy curled up in the seat. The air-conditioning wasn't on, but she felt chilled. Until tonight she'd really thought Cale was making his peace with comedy. She'd tried long and hard to make him see why she loved it. He'd seemed open to what she was doing, willing to try and climb into her world.

What had happened? She didn't know. Probably she'd seen his prejudice evaporating because she wanted to, not because it was. But one thing was sure: even allowing for some sorry-in-the-morning, heat-of-anger rhetoric, the essence of his words couldn't be ignored. She knew everything he'd said tonight was from the heart.

CHAPTER SIX

Sandy's face was being washed with a warm cloth. It tickled. She pushed it away.

Only a few seconds later the cloth was back, cleaning her face more roughly. She rolled away and the washing resumed on her shoulder. Something was tickling her neck. Whiskers. Long dog whiskers.

"Isabel," she whispered. The big tail wagged. "You want your breakfast."

She sat up and put her feet on the floor. She wore her panties and Cale's T-shirt. Her eyes felt sore and she rubbed them. She remembered she'd cried a little in the night. Isabel whined and Milt stood next to her, expectant, but Sandy sat for a minute, thinking back.

Finally she got up and went to the kitchen, stepping carefully as the animals tangled themselves around her bare legs. Through the glass doors she saw what drawn drapes in the bedroom had hidden. The day was wet and dark. She sighed.

The animals were making as much noise as if they hadn't eaten for a week. She got out the dog and cat food and fed them.

A burr of unhappiness was lodged in her throat.

The weather didn't help; heavy clouds shrouded the river, graying the usually lovely vista. But even a cornflower sky and sailboats wouldn't have made a difference.

She'd assumed Cale would take her home last night instead of to Tarrytown. Though they'd fallen silent in the car, exchanging no more angry words, they'd both felt a rift, a harsh vapor of difference.

Probably, she thought as they passed the familiar exit signs, she'd been kidding herself the past month, thinking Cale was coming to like and respect her work. She wanted it so much, she thought she saw it. But he *had* been trying hard. That was no wishful illusion.

Maybe Cale was the one who'd been fooling himself. Perhaps *he* hadn't realized until now that it was a lost cause. Because once the smoke had cleared, Sandy knew—and Cale, too, she was sure—that the heckler incident wasn't the real problem. All the indications of the weeks since they'd met had popped up like mean jack-in-the-boxes, no longer to be glossed over with hope, courtesy, or loving wishes. Cale just didn't care for comedy, despite everything they'd both done, and he was never going to.

She'd still been sorting out these thoughts when she realized Cale had passed the Hastings exit. She'd turned to him questioningly.

"I want to be with you," he'd told her. That had said it all. He knew the rift was there; he didn't like it either. He knew she'd expected to be taken home, that lovemaking wasn't right for now.

When he'd unlocked his door and was trying to

pet both eagerly welcoming animals at once, he'd put his other arm around her and pulled her near.

"All I know is that I want you close to me," he said, and that was how they'd spent the night. No talking, beyond the soothing murmurs of lovers estranged but reaching for comfort. They'd gone to sleep holding hands but otherwise apart, each with troubled thoughts making disjointed dreams.

Sandy had woken a couple of times with her dilemma clear, the night's brittle truth: she couldn't do without Cale *or* her career. But deep within she knew she couldn't keep both, either; couldn't as things were now. What happened tonight would be only the beginning if she tried. Cale would never accept comedy as simply a part of the woman he loved. For whatever reason, his resentment ran too deep. Sandy wasn't sure how much of this he even knew himself yet, but there was no doubt in her mind. She had no more illusions.

Milt was still crunching quietly, but Isabel was done. Her long rosy tongue that had washed Sandy's face had made its final turns around her bowl for crumbs. Now she was panting to go out.

"Thanks for feeding them," Cale said, coming into the kitchen. He squeezed her arm, his hand still bed-warm. He squinted out the glass at the river's pall. He wore only pajama bottoms, and Sandy tried not to look at his muscled chest, the way his back rippled when he reached to smother a yawn.

"Rotten day," she said. As she spoke, the rain suddenly got harder, pelting the terrace with giant drops that splashed up along the glass.

"Do you mind starting the coffee while I walk Iz?" he asked.

Sandy didn't answer right away. Here we are saying all the everyday things people say, she thought, and I feel terrible. I don't want to talk about the weather, or coffee, or the animals. I want to talk about something that'll make me not hurt so.

But there isn't anything.

"Sandy?"

She started. "Yes. I mean no, I don't mind. Go ahead."

The fresh-brewed smell had filled the apartment when Cale and the dog returned, dripping. Sandy ran to the door with a towel for each. They sat in the kitchen with their cups, Sandy still in Cale's T-shirt. She wondered if it was the one he'd worn when she came over that magic afternoon when they'd first made love.

She remembered how she'd been then—mesmerized. She couldn't believe the wonder of the day. She recalled thinking that this was the most happiness she could ever want, the unparalleled delight of those possessive arms and lips, the wonderful things he murmured while he loved every inch of her. She'd never known a man like Cale. No one had ever been able to obsess her so entirely, push everything out of her mind and fill it with himself.

Give him up? Never.

"This is delicious," he said. "As good as mine. You're learning."

She managed a wan smile. "Thank you. O guru."

"What would you like to do today?"

"I guess sunbathing is out."

108

"I guess it is."

This is ridiculous, Sandy thought. He must feel as awkward as I do, and we're talking about domestic nothing, Mr. and Mrs. Suburbia.

She busied herself pouring more coffee, avoiding the sight of him still not dressed, a T-shirt pulled on over his pajama bottoms. His chest hair that she knew the crisp feel of so well spilled out above it. She wished for the heartening comfort of a hug, even an arm around her tense shoulders. Anything but this choppy chatter, this pretense that there was nothing important to talk about.

Cale got up and took eggs, butter, and bagels from the refrigerator.

"I thought we might go to Act Six tonight," he said.

Sandy looked up. "The improvisational theater?"

"Yes. What do you say?"

"Why not?"

He poured beaten eggs into a skillet and put the bagels into the toaster. Sandy set the table.

"As if you couldn't tell I have an ulterior motive," he said. His try at a light tone came out like a cinderblock.

Sandy froze, her hand halfway to the table with a plate.

He said, "Remember what I said last night? About turning your control inward to enhance your performing?"

She nodded. Her breathing was rapid and she felt a feather of panic along her spine.

"Well, I did a lot of thinking during the night."

Welcome to the club.

"This might be an excellent compromise for you to try. If you want to," he added prudently.

Sandy was in motion again, setting the table automatically. Disappointment weighed on her. She'd had a tiny hope that he'd say something like, "On second thought, you really were good last night," and the sun would come out, and everything would be as it had been. Or as she'd wanted to believe it had been. Now that hope was gone, pulverized. Her dilemma was there, it was real, not a bugaboo of the night.

She bit back all the stabbing phrases that rose to her lips. You have two options, she told herself. You can walk out of here right now, tell him what he can do with his "suggestions" about your "art," and drown your sorrows in laughs at Twinkles tonight and every night. Or you can try to meet him partway. The one thing you can't do is politely say no to Act Six and expect him to keep quiet as you go on doing things your way. He already did that. He doesn't want to anymore. He's telling you so very clearly. It's not fair, but it's how it is.

"Would you like to put some forks on the table?" Cale asked gently. She moved out of her trance and got them.

They ate in silence. Wisely, Cale left her to ponder the matter alone. He'd wrestled mightily with himself before suggesting Act Six. He *had* tried to acquire a taste for comedy, and he admired her talent more every day. It was in the clash of those two factors, that the quandary lay. Comedy simply wasn't good enough for her: the nuts who peopled the clubs, the Cro Magnons like Virgil who ran them, the archaic showcase system in which a pro like Sandy performed for cab fare even while pulling down thousands for her out-of-town work. He ached to help her hone her gift in a more worthy medium. He hoped she'd see the sense in that, the *necessity* of it.

Finally Sandy forced a cheerful expression. "I'm willing to go and look," she said.

He grinned and leaned over the table to kiss her.

The rain had stopped by eight, leaving a dripping fog that haloed lights and made the trees crystalline but hung on Sandy's hair and clothes like a wet spider web. Cale had let her out at the Act Six theater and gone to park. She studied the place, trying to picture it as her nightly home, trying to push back her hostility. She'd always felt troupe performers had great skill but lacked the guts to go it alone. Those who can't, join.

The facade was original: a white clapboard front with red shutters and a barnlike double door, with a big fake-crude sign. Just like a summer theater in the country. Cute.

Cale came up Ninth Avenue. In the fading light she could make out his strong thighs in motion.

"Pretty, isn't it?" he said. He put his arm around her and squeezed her shoulders. Not like Twinkles, she finished silently for him. They went in.

There was no curtain. The polished stage was a nice size and contained only a row of chairs. The theater was bigger than Sandy had expected, with about two hundred seats. Nearly all were full. Good for a Sunday.

The house lights dimmed and the actors filed out and sat. They introduced themselves: "I'm Faye, the spunky blonde." "I'm Harry. I'm sarcastic, superior, and gorgeous." "I'm Linda. Your mother would love me."

When all seven were done, they quickly polled the audience for the elements of a foreign fairy tale. Hungarian was the origin suggested. The first cast member began the story, then passed it on. Each one handed it over to the next, sometimes after two sentences, sometimes in midsentence or midword. The pace was quick; nobody faltered. They picked up from each other with smooth expertise, moving in sequence like a circus act. Sandy had to admire the way they all stuck to Hungarian accents, and the fact that most of the tale came from the crowd's ideas. She'd seen so many improv acts that just plugged superficial changes into an established routine.

They couldn't seem to end the piece, though, and she sat back with grim satisfaction. They sure weren't flawless. She'd never let herself ramble that way.

After a few more bits, her trained eye began giving way to enjoyment. She was astonished to realize she was laughing hard, admiring the performance in spite of her prejudice, in spite of what the evening represented. The troupe was superb. While some were quicker than others with funny lines, they were all fine performers, working as a seamless interlocking team.

For their final piece they swapped personas three times. Each traded the image announced at the start for someone else's, even men's for women's. The stunt was breathtaking. Sandy knew how hard it was to establish your real attitude onstage, never mind impersonating others'. She rose with the crowd and cheered.

They went to Jimmy Armstrong's Saloon on Tenth for baconburgers and coffee.

"What did I tell you?" Cale crowed. "That's incredible theater. And you'd be incredible at it."

She looked him in the eye. "I wouldn't stop doing stand-up, though."

He stared back. He was amazed and pleased that she'd capitulated so easily. He'd expected days, weeks, of argument. Dreaded it too. And he wasn't the only surprised one. He could see it in her face: anxiety, uncertainty, and mostly astonishment at herself.

"I wouldn't expect you to," he said, squeezing her hand.

"And," she said, "the big question: Why would they want me? I have no group experience, they don't seem to need another person—"

"I might be able to help out."

Her face went icy. "What do you mean?"

"I know one of the owners. I was thinking I'd just—"

"No way."

"Sandy, be reasonable. You know how these things are. Believe me, you wouldn't get anything you didn't deserve."

She'd been holding her hamburger, not eating it, and now she put it down. "Why do I feel like I'm being shoehorned?"

"I don't know, but you aren't. I'm not waving my cigar and my pinky ring and insisting someone hire you as a hatcheck girl."

"I will stick my head under a bus," Sandy said, "before I'll let you use a connection to force some poor improv actor out so I can get in. That's the scuzziest—"

"Will you relax?" Cale shouted. Several people at the closely packed tables stared. He reddened. He lowered his voice. "If you don't want me to talk to Artie, I won't. But there's an opening. A woman is leaving, the one called Linda. No one would be forced out."

Sandy went back to her burger. "Okay," she said after a minute. "I'll try for it. But only if you keep hands off."

He winced. "If you insist."

"I'll call and ask whether they need anyone. Maybe I'll try to get an audition. But don't expect anything. There are a lot of hungry actors around town."

She made the call late Monday afternoon. Her relief when she got a recording about box-office hours became chagrin when there turned out to be no message tape on it. Lousy luck. She could have left her number, nobody would have returned the call, and she'd have done her duty.

On Tuesday someone answered the phone at the box office. The cheery voice, the same one as on the tape, lost interest when it learned she wasn't buying tickets. No, there were no openings. Yes, she was sure. No, there was no one else who might have more information.

Sandy hung up with satisfaction and made herself two grilled cheese sandwiches.

But when she reported her lack of success to Cale, his face darkened. He was going to call Artie right now. She'd been lied to. Just because some officious airhead was so busy protecting her bosses she didn't have the sense to know she was talking to a professional—

Sandy calmed him. She'd try again herself. She wanted to call Act Six back about as much as she wanted to go hang gliding, but she would *not* let Cale oil the way for her. She'd always prided herself on running her career independently.

Besides, it made her chances of getting into the troupe all but impossible. The word was sure to be out by now. Every comic, plus every good and bad unemployed actor in town, would want the spot. That was probably why the box office was stonewalling. They must be swamped with calls.

"Drop off a resumé and picture. We'll get back to you," she was told with remote courtesy when she finally battled her way through to someone in charge.

She did, and as long as she was there, she gave it a real try. Maybe meeting this wall of indifference had revived her new-comic fighting spirit; maybe she just knew Cale would nag her about improv until she proved it couldn't be done. For whatever reason, she insisted on introducing herself to one of the owners, and did her best to charm him into giving her an audition. He smiled back just as charmingly and repeated that she'd be called to audition if they were interested.

When Sandy phoned Cale a week later to say she had the job, she was more amazed than he could ever have been.

"You really didn't say anything?" she asked.

"I promised, didn't I? No, Sandy. You got it because you deserve it. How do you feel?"

"Mixed."

She couldn't see his face tighten. She went on, "I'm so flattered. I can't believe it. Every time I was over there, even as late as the second callback, they were jammed with actors panting for the job. They were hearing men, too, so the field was huge. And it wasn't just Artie and Sam's decision. After they pared it down to four of us, we each had to work with the cast and let them check us out."

"Wow. You must have been great. What a challenge this'll be for you."

"That's for sure. But the part I don't like is—it's going to take up a lot more time than I expected."

"Why?"

"Rehearsals. Tons of rehearsal time, at least until I get acclimated. I was hoping to fit in at least one late set every night after the Act Six performances. But I don't think I'll be able to. There's still Dan. And you. How much energy will I have for stand-up?"

How much indeed, he thought, but he said, "It'll work out. You'll see."

"Well . . . I hope so."

That'll teach me to try and be cool, Sandy thought, looking at the cast in their neat sporty out-

116

fits. Slacks and open-neck dress shirts, skirts and knit tops, and here was Ms. Professional in jeans older than the solar system and an oversize T-shirt.

"I'm sorry about my clothes. I didn't realize," she said.

"No problem," Sam told her. He and the other owner, Cale's friend Artie, took turns running rehearsals. "I like everyone to dress the way they do for performances, since we're in the unique position of playing ourselves and each other and our own creations, instead of costumed characters. But I think we'll all survive for today."

He patted her shoulder. He was a small, pleasant, unrufflable man, and Sandy liked him. Not like the high-strung theatrical types she'd been afraid of.

"Well, let's see. You're an experienced comic, so no one has to teach you how to move or stand or be quick or funny. That's an easy beginning. The only thing left is teamwork. Let's get started, team."

By the end of the day Sandy felt better. The labyrinth of tricks and techniques and nuances was still elusive, but it was no longer a mystery. She thought she might be catching the edge of what Cale meant about shaping her need to be in control into an artistic self-discipline.

She soon found she'd been right about not having much time for comedy. Since she had to be in the city at ten A.M., she was lucky if she could manage an occasional early set. When she started doing performances, even that wouldn't be possible. She hoped she'd get used to the pace, accustomed to just being busier than before, and fit them in somewhere.

But her days were a challenge. Each rehearsal

pushed her just a shade past what she thought she could do. Progress came fast. The other players were so used to working together that they had a communication she wasn't yet part of, but they went out of their way to include and help her.

After the fifth day, Sam took her aside. "I asked Linda to stay for two weeks while you trained," he said, "but I think you're ready now. What do you say?"

Sandy felt a sudden mix of elation and terror. "I guess so. You're the judge. If you think I am, then I probably am." She swallowed. "Do I look terrified? Because I feel like I'm about to fly a helicopter and run for president while building a skyscraper with my other hand."

Sam laughed. "I'd be surprised if you felt any other way. But you're doing fine. I want to see you blend with the others a bit more, but that'll come. It takes time."

They settled on Wednesday for her debut. Half that day's rehearsal concentrated on Sandy. Over and over she did the exercises: responding to two people talking simultaneously to her without losing either thread; picking a character, situation, and locale out of a hat and portraying the combination; mounting a three-minute entertaining monologue on topics like turtle feet and heating an igloo.

She wouldn't let Cale or Dan come to the performance. She kept to herself beforehand, so anxious she prayed not to pass out. She hadn't eaten all day, couldn't think about it.

But the minute she began she was okay—just the way it'd been when she was learning comedy. A wreck offstage, suddenly confident on. She *was* fine, just as Sam had said. And, as with stand-up comedy, once it was over, she couldn't wait to go back up and do it again.

I'm like an expectant father, Cale thought, checking the door for the ninety-fifth time. Why isn't she here yet? The show ended an hour ago.

And then she was, bursting in the door with her eyes sparkling, strawberry curlicues bouncing around her slim face. His heart lifted. He hadn't expected this. Dejection, a neutral we'll-see expression . . . but not Christmas-morning joy.

"I guess it was a failure," Cale said, holding a chair for her.

She kissed him. "It was great! We had to do an encore, on a Wednesday!"

He stroked her hair. "See what a pessimist you were? You didn't think they'd take you, and they did. You thought you'd never be ready to go on, and you were ready in half the time they expected. You were going to be lousy—"

"But I wasn't. I even had to sign some autographs."

"Is that what took you so long? I almost had a heart attack waiting for you to get here."

"That, and I couldn't get a cab. And Artie wanted to talk to me. How about a drink? My throat feels like a dirt road. And food! Would you believe I haven't eaten all day?"

"No. But I'll pretend to and get you a sandwich." He beckoned a waiter and ordered. "What did Artie have to say?"

"Nothing much. He was very complimentary. I just have to work on my coordination with the others. Listen, can I get a plain club soda before the vodka tonic? Or my throat will—"

"What for?"

"For my throat. I was just telling you." She smiled. "I'm so wiggy. I feel like we're having two different conversations. Speaking of that, remember the piece I told you about, where I have to talk to Phil while he and Harry—"

"I meant your coordination. Why do you have to work on it?"

"Tell you what," Sandy said, laughing. "We'll go to two different tables. You talk about coordination and I'll talk about the piece with Phil. We'll make about as much sense as we are now. Good grief! That's not a sandwich, it's a hubcap."

Cale eyed the mountain of roast beef on rye that had just been served. "Well, you said you were hungry. Can't have you eating the furniture. It costs. Anyway, I really am curious about what Artie said."

"Just—" She swallowed. A quarter of the sandwich was already gone. "Just that I have to keep tuned in more to what the others are doing. Mostly he praised me. He said my presence was excellent, I was really quick, and the audience liked me."

"So that's just a minor point? About the coordination?"

"I think so. Working with others is the one thing I'm new at. It'll take a while."

"And you liked doing the show? It was fun for you?"

"Yes, mother hen. Want some?"

He took a bite of the remaining section of the sandwich.

"The only thing is, I'm not doing enough sets. I'll get rusty."

"No, you won't," he soothed. "You're constantly honing your talent—if not in one way, then in another. Besides, improv is working out better than you ever expected."

She glanced up at him but didn't say anything. How like a non-performer to assume stage time was stage time, no matter what you did with it. She finished the last bits of beef.

He lifted her chin so she had to meet his eyes. "I'm so proud of you," he said softly.

And as always Sandy was caught by the magnetic pull of his power. The silvery eyes explored her face as loving fingertips might. Her skin, pink with the stress and excitement of the evening, dampened. She was afraid the drops would become rivulets and make ugly tracks in her stage makeup.

But Cale took out a large blue handkerchief and began to blot her face and neck. The sensuous motion, his gentle touch, made her warmer, and fresh sweat popped out—not only on her face, but all over. When Cale leaned nearer to dry her chest, she pulled back, startled. Had he forgotten where they were? But he moved insistently closer and finished what he was doing, even sliding the cloth beneath her blouse to dry between her breasts.

She took a quick look around. No one was paying any attention. Good thing. He could have taken off

121

her blouse, pants, and mascara, and she wouldn't have been able to utter a syllable of argument.

Cale tucked the hanky back in his pocket as casually as if he'd been using it to dust off a chair.

"I can't wait to see you," he said.

Sandy was stymied for a minute. "Oh," she said finally. "At the theater, you mean."

"That's what I mean at the moment. I'm not making any promises for two seconds from now."

She smiled. "Soon."

"When?"

"Cale . . ."

"Come on, Sandy. Dan wants to, I want to, Rana, a lot of people. What are you bashful about? I'm sure you're doing a terrific job. There's nothing to be ashamed of."

"I'm not ashamed. This is just so new. I don't feel in the driver's seat yet. I don't know what a bad night is like. I haven't worked a half-empty room. There's enough to get used to without worrying about looking like an idiot in front of my son and my—my—"

"Lover," he whispered in her ear, and bit it.

"Cale, don't . . ."

"When?" he pressed.

"Do you think you could stick some bamboo slivers under my nails instead of this?"

"How about next week?"

"Next week? No!"

"Two weeks, then. Anything that's ever going to happen, happens in two weeks. That's a documented fact. By then you'll be used to it all."

"Where is this fact documented?"

122

"In the *Encyclopaedia Britannica*. Finish your drink. We're leaving."

Why did I say yes to this of all nights? Sandy wondered wretchedly. The Manhattan performer's worst enemy: a Labor Day weekend with a sensational weather forecast. She got up and paced the dressing room, squashing the urge to check the box office yet again. As of five o'clock the house had been only half sold. On any other Saturday they'd be selling seats in the rafters by now.

For the hundredth time she considered telling Cale and Dan not to come. She could leave a message at Cale's club; he was treating Dan to dinner there before the show.

She sat down and swiveled to meet her somber face in the mirror. Sure, she could chicken out. But she'd just have to endure this torture again. And deep down she knew the sparse house was only part of why she dreaded tonight like smallpox. It was the unpredictable element of the whole enterprise that had made her lose her appetite once more.

She'd done stand-up for years before she'd let anyone she knew watch. Even Dan hadn't seen her until she'd been at it so long, she knew each twist in the road—everything that could or would or might happen during a set. By then she'd dealt with rude drunks, waiters taking orders, fire engines drowning her out; having to follow a socko act, a rotten act; she'd even coped with a fire started by a table candle, and a customer having a heart attack.

She was good at improv but lacked the confidence that comes only from experience. The assurance, the aura of being in charge that she'd earned in comedy, wasn't in place. The prospect of Cale and Dan watching her before she had her sea legs was scary enough without the added horror of a bad house.

She checked her watch. Nearly six. Might as well make up. The others wouldn't be back from dinner break for another hour. She needed distraction.

She noticed her fingers were trembling slightly as she stroked on Pan-Cake. She fished through the cosmetics box for concealer to mask the half-moons that seemed to have sprouted under her eyes, and another voice joined the chorus in her head. What, it wanted to know, was she doing working herself into a lather over a new career when she'd already gotten good at something else—something she was perfectly happy with?

She shushed the intruder. She'd been over and over that. Improv wasn't a new career—not like, say, joining the merchant marine. It was simply a broadening of her existing career. She was doing it for excellent reasons. To tramp down the brambles between herself and the man she loved, yes, but not only that. She was heeding Cale's professional advice. The fact that his expertise was the offstage kind only made his judgment more solid. He had the wider perspective that performers had trouble achieving, subjective as they were.

Already she was learning more internal control, thanks to his guidance. It was happening as he'd predicted.

So why do you feel so crummy?

Because I'm *nervous,* as anyone with a brain big-

124

ger than a newt's would be tonight. I like the work, that's the important thing. So take a hike.

A while later the others began filtering back. Their gently joking interplay in the dressing room relaxed her some. When, at ten minutes till curtain, she found the nerve to peek at the house, she was surprised and glad. There were Cale and Dan, seven rows back—and last-minute sales had been good enough to nearly fill the house.

Eight o'clock. A stagehand lowered the dimmers. Follow spots tracked each player as they walked on. "I'm Faye, the spunky blonde." "I'm Harry. I'm sarcastic, superior, and gorgeous." "I'm Sandy. Big mouth, soft heart."

They went into the fairy-tale piece. When the audience was asked for a nationality, Sandy heard Dan's clear adolescent voice call, "Cambodian!" Her cheeks flamed but she joined the others in the Southeast Asian vocal mélange they used for those countries and the bit went well.

She faltered a couple of times in the next routine, a horror film takeoff in which three audience members joined the cast onstage. There was no noticeable error; she simply had to pass the ball when she couldn't think of a good line. But she picked up steam after that, so into her characters she could almost forget Cale and Dan were there.

One of the last pieces called for two TV shows, supplied by the audience, to be combined. Thank heaven Dan had the sense—probably helped by a manly hand over his mouth—not to make another outrageous challenge, and they did "Tonight" with "Family Feud." Sandy's devastating portrayal of

Joan Rivers brought the house down. She beamed with pride as several people shouted "Joan Rivers!" when the audience called for more.

She didn't bother to change after the last curtain call. She took her purse and rushed out. Dan grabbed her in a bear hug but his kiss slid off her face.

"Uk, Mom! They're not kidding when they call it greasepaint," he said, rubbing his cheek. "You were great. Even if you do feel like a crankcase."

Cale grinned. "He's been making cracks like that all night. I wonder where he got the knack?"

"From the stork," Sandy said absently. Why didn't Cale say something about the show?

"He also ate enough french fries to feed a small African nation."

"That's all he had for dinner?"

Dan rolled his eyes. Cale said, "Of course not. He isn't your kid for nothing. He put away two burgers and part of my chicken. And then Rana brought him a piece of chocolate cake I thought he'd never finish—"

"But I did. And Cale's salad too."

They'd been walking up Ninth Avenue as they talked. Now there was a moment of awkward silence that seemed to stretch interminably. A knot was forming in Sandy's stomach. Wasn't Cale ever going to mention the show?

Cale said, "Dan hasn't eaten in three hours. He must be starved. Should we get him some ice cream?"

"No, the only thing we'd better get him is home. He's running a ten-K race tomorrow morning."

"Let's go, then. I'm parked right up here."

"You two can stay in town if you want," Dan said. "I'll catch the eleven-twenty train."

"Thanks, sweetheart, but I'm tired myself." She turned to Cale. "Actually, I should take him up on it, to reinforce the behavior. He's only this accommodating about every fourteen months."

Cale chuckled and took her hand. She wondered if he noticed how cold it was. The ride to Hastings was fairly quiet. Cale and Dan seemed at ease while the hard thing in Sandy's belly grew.

At one point he put a cassette in the player, a Bach toccata. Sandy said, "That's so heavy. I like your piano tunes better."

He shrugged. "Don't want to lose my ear."

"Ear, schmear. Play what you like."

"I like this."

"You do? You look like a kid being forced to eat his carrots."

He frowned in annoyance, but left the cassette. Sandy went back to her uneasy silence.

She invited Cale in. She hadn't wanted to ask his opinion in front of Dan but neither would she let him go without knowing. Dan poured a glass of milk and headed for bed.

"Tea?" Cale said. "I'll make it if you're tired."

She stalled a minute until Dan was out of earshot. Then she faced him, heart thumping. "What did you think?"

"Of the show? I loved it, of course. You were wonderful. You know I'm your biggest fan."

Relief melted through her. How stupid she'd been to be paranoid. She was sure he hadn't liked her, when he just hadn't thought to say what he assumed she knew.

She went to make the tea. Where were those shortbread biscuits with the chocolate? Suddenly she was ravenous.

"Thanks for treating Dan," she said, bringing a tray into the living room. Cale took it and set it on the coffee table. His back muscles bulged beneath his charcoal jacket.

He joined her on the couch. "Oh, I probably had more fun than he did."

"He had a great time. I can tell."

"Good. He loved the show too. You should have seen his face light up every time you got laughs."

Sandy bit into her third piece of shortbread. "That's wonderful to hear. I was so nervous. Hard to believe, isn't it, after six years?"

"Not so hard. You've been performing for six years, but not improv."

"True." She finished the biscuit and poured them both more tea. "I was so unglued I even thought you didn't like the show when you didn't say anything at first."

"Not at all. It's just that, of course, you're still new at this."

Sandy looked up.

"Has Artie or Sam said anything again about that business from before?" he asked.

The knot was back. Unconsciously she put a hand on her stomach. "What business from before?"

"About interweaving with the other players."

"Sometimes. Why?"

"No big thing. I just wondered."

She put down her teacup. "Wondered what? Cale, what's going on?"

"Nothing's going on." He picked up her hand and began playing with the fingertips. "I just couldn't help noticing that you kind of stood out."

"Well, I hope I did."

"Why?" he asked, dropping her hand.

"Why?" She shrugged. "Isn't that the whole point of being a performer?"

"Not if you aren't performing alone," he said patiently.

"Well, we aren't the Rockettes. There has to be originality in improv."

"Naturally." His tone was placating but tension tautened his face. "Maybe not quite so *much* originality, though."

"What much? Are you saying my parts were too far out?"

"No. I'm saying . . . well, 'my parts' sums it up. That's how you seem to see yourself."

Sandy plunked her mug down hard. "So you think I hogged the spotlight."

"No, damn it. You just have to work harder on functioning as a company player rather than on being funny individually."

"Oh. Sorry. Now I see the difference. I only hogged the spotlight somewhat."

"You're ticking me off. You insist on interpreting everything I say—"

"—the way you mean it, instead of letting you twirl me around in circles with your doubletalk. You should hear yourself, Cale! 'Oh, no,' " she mimicked. " 'I don't mean you'd drive over your own grandmother to make yourself look good. I only mean you'd drive over her once or twice.' "

"This is a lost cause," Cale said, standing. "I can't talk to you tonight. It's like trying to make sense to the Statue of Liberty."

"To no one else would what you're saying *make* sense."

"Tell me one thing. If you didn't want to know what I thought, why did you ask?"

"I— You hadn't said anything. It was excruciating, waiting. How would you like to be in that position? Going onstage in front of the person you love for the first time, doing something new, and getting silence?"

"But you asked my opinion," he said doggedly.

"Of course I did! You fixed it so I had to, keeping quiet like that!"

"Well, if you only want compliments, what do you need me for?"

"Don't ask tempting questions."

"Do you want some dingo with a clipboard following you around saying, 'Yes, Ms. Shaw, you're wonderful, Ms. Shaw'? I like to think my guidance is helpful."

"Right now it's as helpful as rabies."

Cale glared poisonously and walked out. She heard the Lincoln crunch out of the driveway as she pounded the wall with the soft side of her fist.

CHAPTER SEVEN

"You were right," Sandy said.

"What? I can't hear you."

"You were *right*," she shouted into the phone. She could barely hear him over the music. "I just—"

"Hold on. I'm going to pick up in my office."

She felt oddly calm as she waited. The initial shock was over. The deeper one hadn't penetrated yet.

"Sandy? Sorry. That's a really loud number. What were you saying?"

"That you were right. About what you told me two weeks ago."

"What do you mean?"

She sighed. It was so hard to say. She couldn't remember ever having to say it before. "I just got— They asked me to leave. Sam and Artie. I stand out too much."

"Oh, love," he said softly. "Where are you?"

"At a pay phone. On Ninth Av— Avenue." Tears spilled out, a lot of them all of a sudden. She still had her makeup on. Fleshy splotches began to dot her blouse.

"I'll pick you up."

"No. I can get a cab. But meet me at the alley door, okay? I look terrible."

On the way to the club she used a whole pack of tissues blowing her nose and wiping off her makeup. She did it in fierce swipes. By the time she arrived, her skin was a mottled combination of pale white and angry red. Bits of blue eye shadow remained. Her face looked like the American flag.

Cale had the alley door open before she was out of the cab. She ran to him as fast as she dared, dodging debris. He pulled her into his office, closed the door, and took her in his arms.

She started to sniffle again. "You must be so disappointed in me."

"Shh. Don't be an idiot." He kissed both cheeks and stroked her hair back. He hurt for her. "You're brave. I love you."

"I feel awful. Humiliated and . . . just awful!" A strand of rippled red-gold clung to what was left of her lipstick. She pushed it away.

He pressed her head to his shoulder. His hands massaged her back, trying to warm and comfort. "You're so talented. And you were enjoying it. I'm sorry."

"Was I? I don't know." He stiffened, so briefly she didn't notice. "I only know I feel like an insect now."

"Were they nice about it, at least?"

She shrugged inside his hold. "As nice as you can be when you're telling someone to take a walk until her hat floats. The worst part was the others. As soon as I came out of the office, they knew. My face must have looked like I died."

132

"Poor love." He kissed the point of her nose.

"I just grabbed my things and ran. I couldn't face anyone. I keep asking myself, what if I had paid attention to you two weeks ago? Maybe this wouldn't have happened. But, you know, part of me did pay attention." She raised her head. "I think I did try to shine less. To be one of the group. And it didn't work."

Tears came again. Before she could wipe them away, Cale was pressing her face to his chest, not caring about his linen jacket. He rubbed her arms, caressed and petted her, as if to make the pain go with his touch. She'd had guts to take this shot—and look what had happened. It was partly his fault. He should have tried harder to help her become integrated. But after the way she'd reacted when he mentioned it, he hadn't wanted to again.

Well, he'd try to help her more now. He'd been glad to have her working in a more dignified setting than that dive next door. He'd find something else, something worthy, where she could shine like a star and nobody would stop her.

Her sobs were easing and he could feel her beginning to soften beneath his hands. She put her arms around his neck and clung in a way she'd never done before. He ached with feeling for her.

He released her just long enough to turn the bolt on his door. Sandy was too dazed to see why immediately, but some deeper part of her knew. Fed by her pain, a river of need began to rise, and when Cale pulled her to him again, she pressed herself as close as she could.

He held her head in both hands and drew back.

Her gray eyes were heavy lidded and puffy, the long lashes a tangle of wet mascara lumps. Bits of orangy makeup were clotted by her hairline. One feather earring was missing, the other damp and flattened. He'd never loved anyone so much.

Some of her Pan-Cake was on Cale's clothes, Sandy saw. There was even a little on his chin, greasy against the trace of a beard. He scanned her face, as if making sure all parts were intact. Love and empathy were in his eyes, and hurt. For himself? Or for her? Or both?

What had she gotten herself into—with Cale, with her life, trying to keep them both happy? Well . . . they were together. She couldn't think much beyond that, but it meant everything. Now more than ever. She'd felt pain like this before. But she'd never shared it. Never thought to; never been asked to.

The need rose again, stronger. Her eyes must have given the message, because she saw his grow smoky. Then the hands behind her head were holding her for his kiss and they tangled in her hair as she responded. She felt his tongue exploring her mouth as his eyes had her face. He was reclaiming his territory, affirming its familiar delights once again.

She missed the closeness when his tongue retreated, and she followed it. She traced the contours of his sculpted lips and touched the corners before entering his mouth. His fingers tightened painfully in her hair. She ran her tongue over the large teeth, behind them; she tasted the ridged top of his mouth

134

and the hidden places under his tongue. She wanted to know his mouth as she did her own.

The river inside her was swelling, starting to dissipate the pain and confusion of the night. A delirious warmth was growing in their place. She blessed the way Cale's hands numbed everything but the rising heat. She'd be happy to stay here for the rest of her future, held in the arms of this man who loved her, wanted the best for her, showed his adoration in the delicious feelings he evoked with his hands and lips.

She felt his fingers on her blouse, finding the buttons and undoing them, though his lips stayed melded to hers. She pulled back.

"Cale, what if—"

"I want to touch you," he whispered, and kissed her again. She had no will to argue. In a moment her blouse was open, then her bra, and he was cupping her soft breasts. She could feel the tension in his hands; she didn't know he longed to hold her harder, show his love in a way his light caress belied. But in his passion he didn't trust himself not to mindlessly harm the delicate skin. To cause her even an instant's discomfort was unthinkable. She'd been hurt so badly tonight.

But he wanted her desperately! He wasn't sure how much longer he could control himself.

Sandy sensed his mounting desire and arched against him. His hands on her bosom flicked fire along every nerve. Barely aware of what she was doing, she dropped her hands to his buttocks to pull him closer still. He groaned . . . and now his hands were less than gentle. But she welcomed it, the pleasure/pain. She was becoming lost in a fog of wonder that was Cale, their love, their hands, lips, and bodies. . . .

Cale pushed her blouse all the way off. He removed his jacket and dropped it. He started on his shirt buttons, his eyes devouring her creamy shoulders and midriff, lingering on her bare breasts. But suddenly he seemed to give up the impossibly complicated task and he reached for her again, dropping kisses everywhere. When his lips found a nipple and gently pulled, Sandy cried out.

The next thing she knew, Cale was leading her to the couch he'd bought to replace the old settee. There was a message in his eyes and hands. Something within her, older and wiser than conscious thought, responded to it. For a long, blazing second she looked back at him, involuntarily signaling her desire that linked with his. Then she was loving him as he wanted, and the pleasure was incandescent for them both.

She wished the joy would last and last, but his body's curled-spring tautening told her the time to savor was now. She loved him totally, letting her feelings guide her, her mind off somewhere else, not needed now. She felt his heat build higher and higher, until surely it could build no more. And then the world was breaking apart for him, and Sandy rode with him along a fiery cascade that seemed to carry them toward the stars.

In a minute he reached for her, his smile full of love. It was delicious to lie in his arms, feel the whole length of him warm against her.

They stayed that way for a while, just holding

each other. Soon Sandy realized she was stroking Cale's thigh. Her hand seemed to have found its way there of its own accord, but she didn't remove it. She liked the feel of the sinew under her palm, and she liked what she saw in Cale's face, the rebirth of yearning.

She wondered how long she could do that, caress his thigh and watch the reactions flick across his face. She felt the muscle tighten a bit, then more. Her own breathing was quickening as embers, never doused, glowed once again. She inched her fingers down a fraction, toward the sensitive inner part of his thigh, and watched his eyes close briefly as he drew in a deep breath. When he opened them again, the passion was back full force. He pulled her on top of him and pressed her near.

Cale's hands running up and down her back, everywhere he could reach, inflamed her. Thighs, buttocks, the fine bumps of her spine jumped to life. The image of what had just happened, remembered sensations of awesome power, danced on her emotional screen. How she loved to love him! The excitement of the feelings she evoked, the way he needed her . . . as they needed each other right now.

Sandy felt strong arms pushing at hers, lifting. She wanted to resist, to stay there, but Cale was insistent. He stood and pulled her to her feet. As fast as his fingers would work, he removed her skirt, hose, and panties, and then started on his own clothes.

For a second Sandy's mind took over, reminding

her where they were. "Cale? I know the door's locked, but . . . someone could knock, or—"

His eyes held hers as he stripped off his shirt. "I don't care."

"What if I do?"

Deliberately he removed his pants and shorts before he answered. "Do you?"

She tried to keep her eyes up, but she couldn't. Now her face mirrored the wanting in his, and it was all the response he needed.

"It wouldn't have mattered," he whispered as he came to her and folded her naked form against his hairy strength. "All that's important is how much I need you now—and you need me. Can you deny it?"

She tried to bring his lips to hers, but he removed her hands from his head and held them. "Well?"

"No."

"That's what matters. I don't want us ever to forget it."

He kissed her, and her lips, her whole being, seemed to melt into him. He couldn't have hidden his impatience if he'd wished to, and the next moment he was pulling her back to the couch. She went gladly. She was shaking in her eagerness for him to be part of her, their oneness complete.

She lay on the couch and reached for him, but he shifted her to her side. His yearning showed in his face, his hurried movements. She longed for him too. Would the moment never come?

At last he lay beside her. He reached to raise her leg, but she was doing that herself, welcoming him. Then the sweet invasion. Immediately she knew, with the speck of her mind still capable of thought, why he'd spent precious moments moving her. His urgency had taken him over. He might have hurt her if she'd been underneath him.

It was the last thought she had. Her sensate self took charge. It pushed her to meet his motions with powerful ones of her own, as driven as he. The wash of need she'd felt from the instant he locked the door became a raging tide. She knew nothing but the force of it. Unaware of her own soft cries, her hands hard all over him, she rushed with him toward a place their hunger compelled them to share.

Cale's hips pounded hers in love's rhythm. His mouth made harsh sounds by her ear but he didn't know he spoke them and she didn't know she heard them. For both there was nothing but the flight to that divine crest. It grew closer, closer. Once again Sandy knew within herself Cale's volcanic joy, and it triggered her, sparking a supercharged interior light show. Her body arched a final time and Cale met it, gripping her as his own sensations descended to a honeyed glow.

This time it was tears of release that slid down Sandy's face. Cale licked them away and cradled her head against his chest.

By Tuesday the pain began to lift. Polishing her nails in the bedroom, Sandy could hear Helen singing in her tuneless, incomprehensible croon as she went about her work—probably adding dust to the furniture. The sound was oddly comforting.

She'd begun to realize that it was the rejection that hurt most, not the fact that she was out of Act

139

Six. She just hadn't been prepared for the knifelike shock of being fired from the troupe.

In fact, her depression had held an element of relief. She didn't have to do improv anymore.

A coppery drop of polish formed on the end of the brush and then fell as Sandy pondered this thought. I *liked* improv, didn't I? I was so excited when I started. So why am I glad I don't have to do it now?

She saw the polish on her dressing table and cleaned it off, pushing the Q-tip like a tiny broom so as not to smear any nail.

The answer was suddenly there: *What I liked about it was that I was performing.*

"Wan' lawnch?" Helen asked from the doorway.

Sandy smiled at her. She'd been so mopey that Helen had started to act like a mother coyote, aggressively protective.

"No, thanks. I'm still full from breakfast."

"Fah. Marconi no good. Stay in your gut." Helen patted her own capacious belly.

Marconi? Oh, the leftover spaghetti she'd finished after her English muffin.

"Leetle senwich?" Helen cajoled. "Tunafeesh? I make nize, with onion."

Sandy shook her head. The phone rang. Gratefully she dashed to answer. It was Cale.

"I'm glad you called," she said. "Helen was threatening to make me lunch."

"But she hates to work."

"She thinks this is an emergency. I've been so draggy. Yesterday she made soup."

"Oh, no. What kind?"

140

"Hard to say. Maybe cream of garden hose. It was white, with rubbery green things."

"You ate it?"

"Of course not. I want to live."

"That's a relief. I wasn't sure about that these last few days."

"I'm coming out of the funk. Speaking of relief— I think that's part of why."

"What do you mean?"

"I'm relieved that . . ." she began, and stopped. She should tread carefully. It had been mainly to please Cale that she'd joined the troupe. He wouldn't want to hear that she was panting to get back to stand-up—that the reason the work had seemed wonderful at first was that she hadn't done *any* performing for a while. She would have loved break-dancing at that point.

"I guess I'm just relieved that I feel better," she finished vaguely.

"Good. Because there's something I want to tell you about."

Sandy waited.

"I mean in person."

"Something you want to tell me in person? That sounds ominous."

He laughed. "Not at all. It's something good. Why don't I come over and we'll take a walk?"

"A walk?" she echoed incredulously, as if he'd said, "a parachute jump."

"Sure. I know you're no fitness nut, but don't tell me you don't exercise sometimes."

She shrugged. "I raise my arm to hail a cab."

"You really never walk, though? Just for the pleasure of it?"

"I guess I do. But not the way you mean. You probably like to hike. Get the old blood pumping."

"Kind of. What do you like?"

"More of a saunter. Maybe stop for ice cream."

He laughed. "Okay. Put on your sauntering shoes. I'll be there in ten minutes."

She spent the time holding her nails in ice water. She'd read that they dried quickly that way. When Cale came, her fingertips were like ten small whitened prunes.

"Ready?" he asked. He wore jeans, not the old ones, but a dry-cleaned pair, and a red rugby shirt. He had some tan left, and the color of the shirt deepened it.

"Yes. Do I need a sweater?"

"Probably." She went and got a bulky cardigan. He laughed. "You don't need *that*. We're going to walk in the sun, not go ice fishing." He went down the hall. She followed him into her room, where he found her sweater drawer on the second try. He pulled out a filmy beige pullover that looked nice with her chocolate pants. "This is what I meant. You could insulate a house with that other thing."

He was right. There was a late-September bite in the air, but the sunshine was warm. Sandy started down the street. Cale stopped her.

"Let's go the other way."

She made a face. "It's uphill."

"Genius," he said, "think a minute. There's an advantage to walking uphill."

She looked blankly at him.

142

"Afterward you get to walk down."

"Ah."

She actually enjoyed it, walking with her hand in Cale's. A few beginning leaves trickled down. She caught the changing-earth smells. Squirrels were noisy in the trees. Something non-squirrel-colored caught her eye, and she turned to see a brown rabbit dash off.

"This is fun," she said with surprise.

"See? Exercise is painless. You'll be ready for pole vaulting before you know it."

"Oh, I almost forgot. What did you want to tell me?"

He grinned. "Let's say I have a consolation prize for last weekend."

"What kind?"

"How would you like to read for a movie?"

"I wouldn't," she said without thinking.

He stopped, dropping her hand. "What?"

She saw his frown and felt foolish. She should have been more diplomatic. It was her old defensive habit of being brutally honest and then some.

"I'm not an actress." She tried to get a chuckle out of him. "The only thing anyone would hire me to do on a movie set is make coffee. And that would only be if Helen wasn't available."

"Will you listen for a minute, instead of turning everything into a laugh? This is no joke."

She started to answer with a dig but made herself say instead, "Sorry."

He took her hand again. "Remember Vince Collins? You met him at my club."

"The producer?"

"Right. He's casting a comedy now. There's a small speaking part he thinks you ought to read for."

Sandy walked along quietly. Rebellious anger gnawed at her. Determinedly she stomped it down. There were so many things she wanted to say—insulting, inflammatory things that would feel satisfying for a minute and then haunt her sleep.

She'd have to try and explain calmly. "The joke was inappropriate, maybe, but I meant it when I said I'm not an actress. It's such a big difference between—"

"Are you serious? Have you forgotten that I've seen you work in a real theater?"

"Improv isn't at all like standard theater work. If it was, I couldn't have done it."

He shook his head impatiently. "The part would be fabulous experience for you. You can't possibly turn down the chance to try for it. No performer would."

Watch this performer, she wanted to say, but willed her mouth shut once more. "Let me explain why it's so different," she said. "When you do stand-up—or improv—you rely on your wits. But in a play or movie you follow a script. I don't—"

"You can pretty well count on a good script. Vince has a clunker now and then, but most of his movies are terrific. Remember *Earmuffs and All?* I never laughed so—"

"You're not listening," she said tightly. "Will you please pay attention to what I'm saying instead of talking at me?"

Grooves appeared between his brows. She could

almost see behind them, to where his sense struggled with his pride as hers had, fighting the urge to snap back.

"Okay," he said finally. "I'm listening now."

Hallelujah. "I was saying that mouthing lines someone else wrote, portraying situations you didn't create, is like the difference between paper dolls and flesh people. If I suggested you try masonry, since you live and work in places made of brick . . . well, that's how close acting is to stand-up."

"Sandy, this isn't *Anna Karenina*. You say 'acting' as though the word only means heavy drama. Do you really think I'd steer you so wrong? I told you, it's a comedy."

"But—" She stopped, searching for another way to make her point. He just had to see.

"You think I don't understand why following a script is the opposite of what you love," he said.

She turned in surprise.

"Of course I realize that. I couldn't be so close to you and miss it. What *you* don't understand is that I'm not talking forever. There's nothing to panic about." He could see how upset she was—holding on to her temper, but not easily. He didn't want to hurt her. He wanted her to be happy. But he owed it to both of them to elevate her work beyond the crummy showcase clubs she thought she needed. Her talent glowed way above that scene.

"I'm not trying to push you into a movie career," he went on. "You should go after this for the same reasons any performer would jump at the chance. The exposure. The experience. Working under the discipline of a director."

"But why do I need those things," she persisted, "if I'm not going to do movies?"

"Oh, Sandy. Now you're just being stubborn. Don't try to tell me nobody but a film actor needs exposure or discipline."

"Let's turn back now," she said abruptly. He looked sideways at her. Maybe he thought her words had a double meaning. Let him. She was sick of feeling like a puppet. "And something else. You said Vince Collins thinks I should try for the part. Did he bring it up? Was it his idea? Or yours?"

"Well, he thought it was a wonderful—"

"Cale." She stopped and folded her arms. "Answer the question."

"I suggested it. But he—"

"I thought so." She started to stalk off.

"Damn it!" he yelled, grabbing her arm. "You're acting like a brat. Try to be grown up about this, will you?"

His outburst was loud on the quiet wooded road. But he was so frustrated. "Every stand-up in town would give an arm for this chance. Sure, you'd rather be asked than have me ask for you. But what difference does it really make? Vince was enthusiastic. That's the important thing. You know that in this business that's almost the same as getting a call. Nobody wastes time being polite when they'd rather say no."

They finished their walk, Sandy deep in thought. Everything he'd said was more or less right. So why did she feel like this? Why had the fall sunshine palled, the sounds and smells of the woods ceased to please her?

And where now, she asked herself as she waved a desultory good-bye to Cale and went into the house, was the lift she'd felt this morning—the easing of the depression that had dogged her since Saturday? She felt lower than ever. After the pummeling she'd taken from her try at improv, the idea of auditioning for a movie had as much appeal as acupuncture. Oh, well, she'd never get it anyway. Everybody and their hairdresser read for these parts. Cale was just so *pushy* about it, that was what angered her.

Helen took one look at her face and said, "You angry heem?"

"You bet I'm angry with him," she said, pulling off her sweater. "He's an overbearing—"

"No, no. You geev *heem* angry?"

"Darn right. I'm not just going to dance to his—"

"No smart." Helen scowled. "Thees man, thees Foller, he fine! He look at you, zzzzz!" She vibrated her pudgy fingers. "He do good honky-ponky, hah?"

Sandy rolled her eyes.

Helen leaned conspiratorially close. "He tell you dance, you listen heem."

This will be the last time I listen to heem, Sandy thought, surveying the entrance to Washington Square Park with dismay. It was a jungle of cameras, lights, tall boom mikes, cables, people, and noise. The pretty Greenwich Village oasis was being overrun with technicians trying to make it look natural. After two weeks of working with these people, rehearsing and then filming, Sandy no longer bothered to wonder things like why a park wasn't natural enough in its natural state. Right now they were using poles to bang on tree branches where her scene would be shot, to make more leaves fall.

"That's too much," the director shouted. "I don't want Jane and Clifton ankle deep in the things. Take some away."

There was another half hour of leaf rearrangement before Collins was satisfied. He'd gone about the task in the way Sandy had learned he did everything, from casting a lead to selecting a Danish— with a ponderous concentration appropriate for a summit meeting and little else. Everyone working on the film was like that. It was a comedy, but the atmosphere was light as granite. When she'd originally read for the part, their response to her had been downright funereal. She'd been speechless when they phoned to say she had it.

"Places, Jane and Clifton," Collins called.

Sandy sat on a park bench with her screen boyfriend, Travis Weldon, who had a sizable supporting part. Light and sound levels were measured. She tried to seem cool and professional and not flinch as all the mikes and meters were stuck in her face and dangled around her head.

Collins hunkered down in front of them. "Let's just recap this sequence," he said. "Jane, I know you've rehearsed it several times, but we were running straight through the script then. I warned you, remember, that since we shoot out of order, you can lose the thread. It's easy to forget what's happening at the point where the scene comes."

Sandy nodded, hiding her annoyance. His insistence on calling the actors by their screen names was bad enough—as if their character personas would vanish in a puff of smoke otherwise. Now he seemed to feel that if he didn't prevent it, she might suddenly think she was riding an elephant in a circus drama.

"You two have had a fight," Collins said. "Remember that scene, Jane, when Clifton calls you a troublemaker, and you say you were only protecting his investment?"

He paused. He was actually waiting to see if she remembered. She nodded again.

"What you're going to do now comes right after that. Directly after it. Follow me?"

This time she wouldn't nod. He'd have to take it on faith.

Collins stood. He was a little red in the face. The squat couldn't be very comfortable, with his jeans that fit like a coat of paint and his paunch pillowing over them. He pushed a hand under his Nevada-shaped belt buckle. Sandy supposed it was digging into his belly.

The distraction seemed to make him forget she hadn't shown whether she understood him so far, and he went on. "Now you've gone for a walk to talk things out, and you're sitting in the park. It's peaceful here—"

It *was*.

"—and you're en rapport, if you catch my drift."

Sandy saw Travis following along intently, his white-blond brows knitted with effort.

"On what?" he asked.

"En rapport. You know, uh, sympatico . . . uh—"

"Together," Sandy supplied.

"That too. So Clifton apologizes, and you apologize, and you both start saying why you got mad in the first place, and before you know it you're arguing again." He interlocked his fingers and held them out. "See how this all fits together, the comic aspect of it?" He didn't wait for an answer, too delighted with his rundown of what they'd gone over and over in rehearsals. "Then Clifton gives his line, 'That does it, you'll never get me to the altar now,' and you jump up and stamp your foot and say, 'Clifton Margulies, I wouldn't marry you if you were the last man on—' "

"Stamp my foot?" Sandy had resolved to live with the trite situations and hackneyed dialogue of the script after her few tentative suggestions had been shot down, but this was a new one. "Isn't that kind of—I mean, I don't think anybody still—"

"It works," Collins said. "Okay, all set? Any questions? Fabulous. Let's—"

"Mirror," Travis said, and an assistant gave him one. He checked his face from all angles. He smoothed a microscopic makeup smudge on his jaw and fluffed his sun-streaked curls. Sandy had decided early on that the nearest he'd ever been to a surfboard was playing a Beach Boys record. He gave the mirror back—she was sure he'd have just flipped it behind him if the assistant hadn't been there reaching—and they were ready to begin.

"I shouldn't have yelled, Jane," Travis said. "I'm sorry.

"I'm sorry, too, sweetheart. Let's not yell at each other ever again."

"That's great by me."

"It was just that . . . well . . . I was only trying to help." She looked at him, trying to get a communication going, some contact that would help them play their parts realistically in spite of the clichéd dialogue. But it was the same as in rehearsals, when she'd tried to find a connection in his eyes. Like looking out a plane window. Nobody there.

They finished the scene. Collins wanted another take. Travis called for the mirror again and insisted on being powdered. They did it three more times.

Maris Barker, the female lead, arrived during the last take. She watched absently. When it was done, Sandy heard her say to Collins, "Don't let her stamp her foot. It looks ridiculous. This isn't the Roaring Twenties."

"Right," Collins said, as though she'd just reported a cancer cure. "Jane, sweets, that'll have to go, that foot stamping. Sorry. Let's take it once more."

CHAPTER EIGHT

"And then he had the gall," Sandy said, "to pretend it had been *my* idea to stamp my foot! When he told me to do it, nobody heard except Travis, and Travis doesn't remember which hand to shave with. But when he said not to, as if he was disappointing me, *everybody* could—"

"You're not eating your burrito," Cale said. "Look, I'm sorry this turned out to be such a bomb. I wish I knew what went wrong. I don't know Collins that well, but he's had some hits."

"Well, he must have used a ghost director. The man has the IQ of an eggplant."

"I hope you won't let this sour you on movies."

"Are you serious?"

"Of course I'm serious."

"That's like advising a dead pedestrian to keep jaywalking." She dipped her burrito in guacamole and took a bite. "This is delicious. Good old Armstrong's. I'm glad we came here. It's just what I need."

"You really wouldn't try another movie?"

"Would you dive into a pool that had no water?"

He stirred his coffee. "These remarks are a little out of proportion, don't you think?"

"No. What I think is that I've been a good sport, following your . . . guidance and trying these things you suggested." She considered changing *suggested* to a more honest word, but refrained. "I tried hard, Cale." Her voice went softer. "I know how you felt—feel—about stand-up. But nothing else is working."

He scowled. "You are a good sport, but you have to give it a little more time. Take my word for it. I've been managing performers for fifteen years. I'm sure we'll find something that's for you."

"I know what's for me. After we finished up shooting today, I couldn't wait for night so I could do a set. I've done so few lately I was nervous, but when I got up there—well, I just felt more sure than ever that that *is* my art. You wanted me to rechannel the qualities I use in comedy. I worked like crazy at it. But it didn't happen."

She sat back, dropping her hands to her lap so the shaking wouldn't show. Confronting him was nerve-racking, but she felt more contentious than she had in a long time, determined to say her piece.

Cale had never given her an ultimatum; she didn't really believe he'd say "It's me or comedy," but she didn't see him accepting it either. She didn't know what would happen. All she knew was that things couldn't continue as they were.

Since August she'd been resigned to Cale's dislike of stand-up and had done everything possible to compromise. Giving *him* an ultimatum—love me, love my work—was unthinkable. She was his, he was hers. It was a solid fact, like tree roots in soil. But nothing was working. She just didn't fit into

153

the space he was trying to carve for her. What could she do? She only hoped her efforts to bend in his direction had softened his attitude.

Cale studied her over the rim of his cup. Frustration and anger roiled in him. Now what? He didn't want her back riding the showcase circuit. It was the worst thing for her. Was that all there was left? It didn't seem fair. All he'd tried to do was upgrade her opportunities, and look what had happened. She acted as if he'd tried to push her into selling refrigerators.

In the back of his mind was a small piece of a fantasy, one he preferred not to look at too closely. He saw himself introducing her to people as an actress. His love, the actress. But he pushed that away. It was beside the point.

"I just thought of something," Sandy said. "I've been back there so irregularly I forgot. Whatever happened with your idea about buying Twinkles?"

"Nothing. It's still up in the air."

"How come?"

He shrugged and looked away. "Just . . . haven't done anything about it."

She was quiet, turning that over. Her coffee toffee pie came and she started on it.

"Does that have anything to do with me?" she asked.

He shrugged again and twisted in his seat to signal for more coffee.

"You've been holding off on purpose, haven't you? To throw me a fish."

"No," he said with aggrieved patience.

"I don't think I believe you. And I don't think I like the whole business."

He grimaced. What the hell did she want from him? He hadn't gone further on the Twinkles deal because he just hadn't, that was all.

"The only reason you don't," he said, trying not to yell in the crowded restaurant, "is that it wasn't your idea. I remember when my not buying Twinkles was a big cause with you. Now, okay, I leave the place alone, and what happens? It's not a shot you happen to be calling at the moment, so you don't like it."

"As shots go," she said quietly, "that's a cheap one."

Something in him wouldn't stop yet. "Is it? I don't think so. You can't stand to give up control. You have to have the upper hand."

Me? she shouted. "Have we been having two different relationships? That must be it, because I'm sure not having the one you just described. Where have you been, Cale, in a submarine? I don't try to grab the reins anymore."

He was sorry for his outburst but not enough to back off entirely. "Well, not as much. But you still do it."

"Are you kidding? *You* have the reins, the horse, and the carriage."

"That's not true. We have a pretty balanced relationship."

"Only by your definition." Her voice was rising again. "I follow all your ideas about changing my whole career, and you follow mine and get soft contact lenses. That's your idea of equality."

155

"Shh," he said. "Okay, I'm sorry."

"It's bad enough that I jump through every hoop you hold out. But then to be accused of calling all the shots—"

"Calm *down*." He gripped her wrist. "We're both on edge. I didn't mean that stuff. Come on, have some more coffee."

She sipped the cinnamony brew. After a few minutes her mind stopped replaying his unfair cracks.

"You had a lousy day and I made it worse," he said as they got into the Lincoln. He pushed back a rippled strand that fell over her cheek. "I love you. I don't want you to be unhappy."

It was moments like this that reminded her with a certainty that sometimes got lost in frustration why she had endured all these changes. She held his face in the semidark car and looked at it, at the familiar planes and creases she loved. She ran a finger along his thorny jawline.

"You're special, Sandy. I want people to see how special. That's why I keep trying to find the right direction."

She wasn't sure that made sense, but she didn't care. The rumble of his voice was reassuring and thrilling all at once.

He bunched her thick hair in one hand and lifted it off her neck to kiss her there. His lips were warm pillows. She rested her head on his chest and his fingers replaced his lips, kneading. They rubbed her neck, the tight muscles beneath, and worked their way down her back.

He was right. She'd had a lousy day and he made

it worse. But she was feeling less like a pincushion now as his hands released her tension inch by inch.

"Sandy . . ." he whispered.

She lifted her head, unwillingly relinquishing the buttery warmth of his cashmere sweater. "Mmm?"

"I . . . uh . . . I love you."

"Mmm." She snuggled back down.

He'd been about to say something else instead. It was an offer he'd hoped to avoid but had always suspected he'd have to make sooner or later . . . preferably later. The idea was disquieting.

But she needed it *now.*

"Sandy."

She nuzzled his neck. "I know. I love you too."

He held her closer. It was hard to get the words out. But he could make her so happy.

"Sandy," he said again, and this time she pulled back. "Maybe it's time you tried working for me."

She looked heavy-eyed, foggy. "For . . . ?"

"On a club date somewhere. Maybe Jamaica. Rana has a three-night show there the weekend after next. You could open for her."

Now she was alert. "You mean it?"

"I . . . yes. Of course I do."

"But you never use comics to open."

He forced a grin. "Then it's time I started."

Her pulse raced with excitement as the reality began to sink in. "It's— I'd love to! But what made you—"

"Hush." He kissed her gently to close her mouth. Now that he'd taken the giant step, he needed some quiet time to get used to the idea himself. "It just

157

seems to me that I ought to put my money where my mouth is."

Noble words, Fowler, he reflected as he pulled up in front of Sandy's house at seven Friday morning.

She opened the door and signaled that she'd be out in a minute. Something in the swirl of her hair, her big smile, reminded him of the steaming July night when he'd first seen her. She'd been something to reckon with, this fiery woman who stood eye to eye with him. It was hard to remember now at what point he'd known there would be more to this than a street argument, but it had certainly been long before the night was over, before he'd come into Twinkles. Her face, her long, lithe shape, her pewter eyes were emblazoned within him perhaps from the first instant.

Now, as the few remaining leaves blew in the morning quiet, he was about to do something he never would have predicted. A comic/singer act— he hadn't thought he'd see the day.

The door opened again, Sandy came out, and his heart remembered why he was doing this. He took her suitcase and put it in the trunk. He could feel her excitement as a palpable thing in the car.

When they stepped off the 727 in Jamaica, the breeze was very different. Moist and soft . . .

Like that first night in the city, Sandy thought. The New York mugginess came back to her for a minute. She recalled the dirt blowing, Cale's streaming eyes. The hot onion loaf. The bland dust-and-plaster smell of his office. The jumble of feelings—high and low, hot and cold.

Well, the evening could have been a dress rehearsal for the next few months. But it looked as though things were going to be a bit different now.

The tropical smell hit her, a blend of flowers, sugary fruits, and the sea. She smiled. She was still smiling when they got to the hotel.

"Rana left a message that she's at the pool," Cale told her after he'd gotten their key. He noticed her face and couldn't help smiling back. "You look happy."

"I am. I'm thrilled to be here. In Jamaica, and working with you."

"Well, me too. Let's go up and unpack. I have some things to check with the entertainment people . . . and then maybe we could go for a swim?"

They spent the afternoon by the pool with Rana, changed, and met her in the dining room for an early dinner.

"Are you eating?" Rana asked Sandy as they were seated.

"Yes. Always."

Rana chuckled. "I thought I was the only one."

"No, there are two of you," Cale said. "The only performers in the Free World who have no trouble packing it away before a performance."

"It's nice to be working with you at last," Rana said. "Took Cale long enough. Or don't you like to mix business with you-know-what?"

"I don't care," Sandy said.

Cale was deeply interested in his melon.

"You'll have a good time. Cale's the best manager I ever had."

Now he looked up. "Thanks, Rana," he said, touched.

"I wouldn't say it if I didn't mean it. I'd have terrible stage fright," she told Sandy, "if it wasn't for him. Anyway, I love having a comic open. I'm excited. I haven't seen you work since the last time I watched you at Twinkles. Tell me what material you'll be doing toward the end, so I can be set."

Sandy took the last spoonful of her conch chowder. "Let's see, you'll know I'm around the middle when I do the piece about men who think they love women without makeup. It takes an hour in front of a mirror to achieve that . . . they wouldn't know the natural look if it bit their ankle, et cetera. . . ."

Rana nodded. "I remember it."

"Then I do some impressions I don't know if you've seen—Ed McMahon and—"

"You do Ed McMahon?"

Sandy grinned. "It's a killer . . . she said modestly."

"And Cher and everybody," Cale said.

"Ugh. He wants me to do all the showbiz ones."

"What for, Cale? If Sandy can be that original, why have her do what everybody does?"

"Oh, he's probably right," Sandy said. "He knows this type of crowd better than I do. I've hardly worked the islands at all. Anyway, there are a few more pieces after that, and when I go into the bit about sportscasters—how they interview the players, and the players always say the game's all mental while they're holding up their incomplete

160

fracture of the elbow with the other hand—you'll know I'm near the end."

They finished dinner and looked over the empty night club. Cale stayed behind to test sound equipment while Sandy and Rana went up to their suites to change. Sandy was laying her clothes out on the bed when he came in.

"Everything okay?" she asked.

"Fine. You'll like the mike. No distortion. And they're all set up for Rana's band. It should be a good show."

She put her arms around him and nuzzled his ear. "I know it will. I'll make it good for you."

She felt the rumble of his chuckle through his chest. "That I'll definitely look forward to," he said.

"I meant the show."

"What show?"

She pulled back, laughing. "Keep away. You can't muss my face."

He went into the sitting room and read while she got ready. He'd put a Beethoven sonata on his tape deck and its restful notes filled the rooms. He happened to look up as she was pulling her cherry-red dress over her head. He said, "Wait. What about the black?"

"I thought this would be better for tonight. It's more—"

He came into the bedroom. "I told you to bring the black."

She hated his abrupt tone. "I did bring it. I just thought—"

"Fine, then wear it."

"Cale! Don't talk to me that way!"

His shoulders lost their rigidity. He turned away. "I'm sorry," he said to the wall.

"What's the problem? You're acting like you're the one who has to go onstage." She saw his body tense again, and she laughed to lighten her words. "Come on. Where's that stageside manner Rana was talking about?"

He turned back to her. "This is new for me. I must be a little jittery."

"A little? You look like you're about to do the Nile in a canoe."

He managed a smile.

"I thought I'd wear the red and keep the black for tomorrow, since it's more formal. Saturday night and all."

"That's why I want you to wear it tonight. A sedate look for your introduction."

She looked sideways at him. What kind of gobbledegook was that? She gave it one last try. "I'm all made up for the red."

He came nearer and studied her. "It's fixable. Tone down the brown eye shadow and make it grayer."

"But then I'll have to change my—oh, all right," she said, giving in as she saw his face begin to tighten. It wasn't worth waging war over. The last thing she needed on an unfamiliar stage was to have her belly doing backflips because of a fight.

Only the usual butterflies were there shortly before ten when Sandy and Cale went down for the first show. He took a front table in the room while she joined Rana backstage. The band was already in place. They'd play her on while an offstage announcer introduced her, and then leave until Rana's set.

Rana squeezed her arm. "Did you see that room? Packed to the woodwork. Nervous?"

Sandy nodded. Rana tried to take her hand, but she snatched it away. "Don't touch. Look," she said, showing her the palm.

Rana peered at the list of words and phrases inked on her skin. "What—oh, your set!" Sandy nodded. "Well, aren't you something. That's a new one. Those few words really help?"

"Sure. If I get thrown for some reason, I can forget when I was born, never mind my material. A word or two brings it back."

She studied the willowy black woman. She wore a silvery satin pants outfit. A tiny rhinestone was pasted near the corner of her eye. Her coffee-cream face was dusted with glitter, highlighting its fine planes. "You look beautiful."

"You think so? Thanks." She grinned. "You won't send anyone away screaming yourself. What did you do to your hair? It looks like gold clouds."

"That's the sun."

"If you could bottle it and sell it, you'd make a fortune."

"Well, I'm glad something sparkles. I don't feel right in this outfit. I was all set to wear red, but Cale asked me not to."

Rana shook her head. "Don't worry. You're dynamite in black. I can't imagine why he's carping about what you wear, though."

"He's just on edge. This is a new way to go for him."

163

"And high time too. Never mind him. I'm so happy you're here, instead of some singer in elevator shoes with laminated hair."

"Is that what you usually get for an opener?"

"That or a group. Crew cuts and tinfoil pants. And that's just the girls."

The band began to play. Rana hugged her. The announcer sang out her name, there was applause, and she was on.

She let the noise wash over her in thrilling waves as she bowed deeply at the end of her set. Her sun-blazed curls touched the floor.

"More!" someone called, and then there was a chorus, and she did another two minutes. When she ran off, the applause followed her. Rana was waiting, grinning as widely as she was. They clasped hands for a second before Rana strode on.

Her set was a hit, too, and the second show went as well. The weekend followed in kind. By the time Monday came, Sandy felt she could conquer the world.

She was pleased with the way she'd performed—but she was proud of how things had gone with Cale too. They'd both had reason to be tense. Cale was trying something he'd never done, never wanted to do; Sandy felt the extra pressure of justifying it. Several times tension had threatened to erupt into a verbal scuffle and they hadn't let it.

She'd bitten off a defensive retort more than once when he'd surprised and annoyed her by suggesting little changes in her material. When she made herself consider the ideas—after all, he had a vested

164

interest now—she found she sometimes agreed. In any case, she was glad she could at least listen. There was a time she would have yelled first and asked questions later.

"Considering everything, it was a success," Sandy said. They were getting on the plane to come home.

"The show? It certainly was."

"Not just the show. The whole weekend. Us. Everything." She smiled up at him from her seat. He didn't see. He was busy stuffing their coats into an overhead compartment.

He settled down next to her. He took the airline magazine from the seat pocket and began leafing through it. Sandy grabbed it and put it back.

"Hey."

"Oh, you don't want that." She took his hand in both of hers and kissed it. "Talk to me instead."

He chuckled. He'd been irritable, but her mood was infectious. "What about?"

"You're asking me, O silver tongue?"

He looked at her nestled in the high seat, her hair a flaming spill of curls over her shoulders. Gold wisps half covered her small face. Her nose was starting to peel. He leaned over and licked her lips. Her mouth opened and he kissed her fully, pressing. His tongue moved inside and met hers.

A glow of heat began. His hands tingled, wanting more of her. He felt a feathery touch at the back of his neck, and then her hand firm on it, pulling him closer still.

He gave himself over to it for a minute, to the delight of her smooth tongue tangling with his, following it home, touching the chip in his tooth. Then

165

he broke away. He watched her face. Her lashes were golden fans. Her skin was a little pinker now.

"And he can talk with it too," she murmured.

He grinned and sat back.

"So. What do we do for an encore?" she asked, her eyes still closed.

"If you can restrain yourself until we're in private, I have several—"

"No." She giggled. "I'm talking about performing."

He came back to earth with a thud. Sandy opened her eyes to find him scowling.

"Oh, dear," she said. "I guess I broke the mood."

He squeezed her hand but said nothing. He didn't know why he looked like that either. But the edginess was starting to build again.

"I'm trying to figure out what direction to take now," she said. "I know you want me to spend less time in the showcases."

He nodded. "It'll be good for you. Less showcase work, more of the kind you just did."

She shrugged. "Then why don't we start right at home?"

It was a full thirty seconds before he realized what she meant. "Caleb's?"

"Of course, Caleb's. I've never asked before because of how you feel about comedy. But this weekend broke the ice, didn't it?"

He was silent.

She sat up and faced him. "The shows went beautifully. You know they did. You gave it a chance and—"

"Fasten your seat belt, please," a passing flight attendant said.

Sandy reluctantly sat back and put it on. "I know how nervous you were. I'm not blind. But whatever you were afraid of, it didn't happen, did it?"

"No," he said.

"So why not use me at Caleb's to open for Rana?"

He couldn't think of an answer that wasn't revolting. Because I want to make you happy, but not that way. Because I love you, but I still hate what you do. Because even good comedy is sleazy, and I don't want sleaze in my club. Because it makes me squirm to watch you do it, even though you're so good. Because—

"All right," he said, amazing himself.

"Oh, Cale." She started to jump up, got caught by the belt, and yanked it open. She hugged him fiercely as the plane started to move. "I'll make you glad. You won't be sorry you said yes."

CHAPTER NINE

Cale looked at the reservations book. Both shows were booked solid. Not surprising for a Saturday, but this was supposed to be a slow month. Usually things didn't perk up until closer to Thanksgiving, when a lot of vacationers were in town.

He'd been asking himself all week why he'd given in. It was simple, really. Sandy wanted this, and he hated to say no. Of course, he'd known immediately it was a mistake. An out-of-town gig was one thing; that was hard enough. But comedy in his own club?

And she had a right to expect this. She'd been flexible about trying what he recommended, avoiding the showcase scene she loved. She was entitled to what *he* could give—including a spot at Caleb's.

Well, it was only one night.

And then what? How would he justify telling her, while they stamped and whistled and screamed for more, that she couldn't work here again? Yes, darling, you should stay out of the showcases, but no, I won't make my room available to you.

The phone rang in the silent club. He felt reprieved, and then foolish. It took about twelve seconds to turn down the reservation request, and then he was back between his rock and hard place. What was he going to do? He loved Sandy more every day. He wanted to help her. But there was some-thing about having regular comedy here, something he couldn't swallow. It was a kind of final capitulation. Not to Sandy, but to . . . the opposite of art, whatever that was. To bring in comedy was to cancel out art.

It was just after eight when Sandy parked the Honda around the corner from the club. The sunny November day had become a frigid night, and a cold gust whipped her hair when she got out of the car. Leaning against the wind, she made her way to the club.

She pushed the door open, looking for Cale. There he was, just coming out of the kitchen.

"I'm so excited," she said. She took off her coat. "How are the reservations?"

"We're full."

"Both shows?" Cale nodded. "Wow."

Rana came in and she and Sandy went to the dressing room. Sandy was just as glad to be out of Cale's way. It was understandable that he seemed distracted, but she didn't want his mood to affect her.

"Well, this is some red-letter night," Rana said. She was leaning toward the wall mirror, touching up her blush.

"I just hope it goes well," Sandy said.

"You're not under pressure or anything, are you?"

"Nah. What a silly idea."

They didn't say anything for a while. Sandy took

deep breaths and tried to relax while she changed her clothes and fixed her makeup.

Finally Rana said, "I don't want to make this any harder for you. I just want to say that I have some idea what's going on, and I'm on your side."

"Thanks. I'm not sure you're saying that to the right person."

"I'm not sure either. But he's on his own."

Sandy smiled wanly into the mirror. She could see Rana's eyes, foxlike, looking sideways at her.

"Just be loose," Rana said. "It'll work out."

"Keep telling me that."

There was a knock, and the sound man called, "Five minutes." Sandy ran a brush through her hair a final time, smoothed her green dress, and got ready to go on.

She forced herself to stay cool when it started to go bad, to focus on what she was doing and not look at Cale or Rana. Her act continued on automatic pilot while she considered her options. She could try a cheap shot—a dirty joke or a drug line. She could acknowledge in a funny way that she was bombing; it might clear the air and gain the audience's support. Or she could abandon her material and just work with the crowd, using her wits to score off whatever they gave her.

She chose the third, and started a conversation with a sympathetic-looking man at a front table.

"What do you do?" she asked. He gave a long-winded answer about chemical engineering, and she said, "Would you mind repeating that? I dozed off." That earned her first real laugh of the night, energizing her. She bantered with him some more and was starting to build when she suddenly remembered that Cale wanted her to downplay the audience stuff. She tried to cover her frustration but the crowd sensed something, and her slight hold was gone. She couldn't get them back.

She finished the set with as much dignity as she could manage. There were no belly laughs, but this was a music audience and they were polite. At least she didn't leave the stage feeling as though she wanted to crawl under it.

She looked perfunctorily around for Cale and wasn't disappointed not to find him. She hurried to the dressing room. The hot lights, combined with her nerves, had mussed her face. She went to work with brushes and pencils. She used the time to give herself a pep talk, do what she could to keep the second set from repeating the first. She hoped Cale wouldn't come into the dressing room. It was hard enough to get her energy up after a lousy set. Having him there would only increase the pressure she felt.

She pulled out every trick she knew for the second show, but it was even worse. This time she *did* want to slink off and hide. It took colossal effort to join Cale at the house table after her smattering of applause that was barely the courteous minimum.

Cale took her hand when she sat down. She kept her face carefully neutral. Fortunately, she didn't have to talk for the next thirty minutes. She listened to Rana's soothing voice and tried to let it ease the ache inside her.

It didn't help. Nothing would. The situation was

just too awful. She didn't know where she found the courage to sit here, to face Cale and everyone else.

Rana finished her last song and did one encore. When she came to the table, Sandy invited her to sit; anything to put off talking to Cale alone. But Rana just gave her a hug and went to the dressing room.

"I'm so sorry," she told Cale when the silence had begun to throb. She couldn't look at him.

"Don't be silly," he said, but his voice held a hollow note that made her turn. She tried to catch his eye, to see his face, but he was looking around the room, his attention on several other things.

He's avoiding me, she thought. She began to get angry. A minute later she decided she was being paranoid. What did she expect? This had to be every bit as painful for him as it was for her. He had even more reason to be embarrassed.

People were stopping by the table to say hello. Every time someone carefully avoided mentioning her performances, Sandy died a little more. She wished she could go home. In fact, that was just what she *was* going to do. She'd been brave long enough. She got up.

"Where are you going?" Cale asked.

"Home. This is too embarrassing. For you, too, I know."

"Not at all," he said, but she was right. And probably because he felt guilty that he wanted her to go, he insisted she stay.

"Have something to eat, at least," he coaxed.

She let him order her a sandwich she didn't want. She was quiet, not wanting to discuss her disaster

172

and not willing to talk about anything else, but Cale chatted away about one thing and another. He was probably trying to relax her but it had the opposite effect. Finally, tired of waiting for the shoe to drop, Sandy said, "I guess we should talk about it."

He shrugged. "What's to talk about? You had a bad night. It happens."

"Not to me, not often. I have the control to avoid a bad set."

He shrugged again, clearly uncomfortable with the topic. But now that she'd begun, Sandy couldn't stop.

"If I could just figure out what went wrong, I'd feel a little better. At least it won't have been a total waste. I'm going to listen to the tapes as soon as I get into the car."

"Sandy, drop this, will you? You're making things worse. You should try to get your mind off it."

"No," she insisted. "Believe me, after all these years I know when to—"

"And if you have to talk about it, at least stop that pretentious analysis stuff."

She wasn't sure she'd heard right. "What?"

He looked away. "Forget it."

She knew she should listen to that. His face, his voice, every signal told her she'd be foolish to press the issue, any issue, now. But her feelings were screaming for an outlet.

"Did you say 'pretentious analysis'?"

He turned back to her. "Yes. I'm sick and tired of the whole pretentious idea of the mystique of comedy." His voice shook with mocking contempt. "Tape recorders, attitude, the dynamics of a room

—as if this was some precise art. How much of a mystique can there be if I was able to succeed at it myself with no experience?"

Had she stepped into some nightmarish movie? She had no idea what he was talking about. "Succeed at it? What do you mean?"

"That line I wrote for you in Jamaica. About how much you enjoy parenthood."

"You suggested 'compared to electrocution' instead of 'compared to a forest fire.' You call that writing a line? And what does it have to do with anything?"

"It works every time you use it. It even worked tonight."

"So what?"

"So what, yeah, that's the point!"

Sandy paused, replaying his words. "Let me make sure I have this straight," she said then, using every last ounce of control to keep her voice low and steady. She felt as if she'd just banged her thumb with a hammer and the pain hadn't hit yet. In a minute, she knew, the hurt would well up and cover her. "You're saying, 'Comedy is easy—see, I did it with no hands. Therefore, your whole career is a bunch of phony, pretentious garbage.' "

"Well, you don't have to put it—"

"I must be a moron! How could we have come this far without my knowing? It's not that you just don't care for comedy—you *despise* it! And you put me, as a comic, in the same category! You think I'm a clown! A fool!"

"Don't take it so—"

"Stop trying to shush me!" The words came out in

a near-wail as she began to feel the true depth of her misery. It was as if her eyes were being forced open. Words crowded her brain, things he'd said and she'd ignored or covered or assigned an innocuous meaning to.

She'd cooperated in her own deception. She'd probably even masterminded some of it. Cale had never tried that hard to hide his dislike of comedy. She'd wanted the truth to be otherwise; she'd been eager to believe he respected what she did but merely wanted to alter its direction slightly.

Now it was clear how she'd had to push for every small victory. She was so used to doing that, it was nearly automatic. Like someone who thinks a Frenchman will understand English if it's spoken loudly enough, she'd blindly assumed Cale would get to like comedy if he kept watching her do it, once she'd tried the other things and they hadn't worked. If she'd really had his support, she wouldn't have needed to push. *He* wouldn't have pushed *her* so hard away from what she really wanted. And she wouldn't have had to ask to work at Caleb's. He would have offered, long ago.

Once before, she'd come nose to nose with his real feelings about comedy—that night here at Caleb's when she'd first met Rana. She'd left spitting fire . . . and, later, had forgiven the rotten things he'd said.

But that was then. They'd been through so much together since. All the growing—or so she'd thought . . . trying to bend to each other's sensibilities, compromising. . . .

Cale couldn't have been more cruel in the way

he'd picked to insult her tonight. To hear those knifelike things was so different now. Unbearable. Unforgivable.

Enough. Too much reality pressing in at once. She jumped up from the table and headed for the dressing room.

There was an ache behind her eyes, but she wouldn't give in to tears, not yet. The room was empty; Rana had gone. She tried to concentrate on changing out of her dress but her hands weren't working well and the task took a lot of time. She looked in the mirror and barely recognized the stricken face there. She'd almost forgotten how it felt to hurt this much.

"So here you are," she heard him say, coming into the room. She turned and fresh pain shot through her. That face, that voice, all parts of the man she loved . . . and hated. This man who, after letting her believe he loved her for everything she was, had pulverized her with one hideously revealing comment.

"Leave me alone," she said in a choked voice.

He rolled his eyes. "Come on, Sandy. I'm sorry I hurt your feelings but—"

"Hurt my feelings?" Now she couldn't stop the tears. "Is that all you think you did?"

"Aren't you making a bigger deal out of this than it deserves?"

"That wouldn't be possible, Cale! It's about as big as it can be! You've just made it clear that we can't have a relationship!"

He paled a little, but said, "You're going to push this all the way, aren't you? You want me to crawl."

"The only place I want you to crawl is out of here and away from me." With shaking fingers she wiped the streaks of tears and makeup from her face.

"Would you mind telling me what unspeakable thing I did? I know you had a tough night, and maybe I should have been more sensitive, but this wasn't easy for me either."

"You really don't know?"

"No, damn it! And I don't want to play guess-my-trauma."

"Then stop guessing and start remembering. You can manage it, Cale, it was only ten minutes ago. You blew my whole career away with one remark."

"Oh. Well. You're making too much of what I said. It's only because you're upset—"

"Is it? Do you deny you have no respect for comedy?"

"Stop putting words in my mouth."

"If I'm wrong, tell me what you really think," she challenged.

He held her gaze, but said nothing. It was the most eloquent answer he could have given. There was nothing more for either of them to say. She stuffed her green dress in her bag. He grabbed her arm when he saw she really meant to leave, but she shook him off and ran out.

Helen leaned out the back door. "Hev dessert?" She was holding a dish of something red and slithery. Like Jell-O, only more so. Sandy didn't want to look any closer.

"No, thanks," she said. "I'm still working on my sandwich."

177

Helen retreated, and Sandy went back to her contemplation of the bare trees. They looked the way she felt: stark, empty. It was fairly warm on the back porch in the sun, but still, with her cold, she probably shouldn't be out here.

She didn't want to go in, though. Reminders of Cale were all around. At least out here she could empty her mind, think of nothing but the crows and starlings and squirrels, busy in the fading grass.

She pulled her heavy sweater tighter around her and picked up her sandwich. She made herself take a couple more bites, but her nose was so stuffed she couldn't taste. The bread and ham were like cloth in her mouth. Now I know why animals won't eat when they're sick, she thought. You forget what you're doing it for.

She heard the phone and Helen's heavy steps as she went to answer. She hoped it wasn't Cale, but it didn't really matter. He'd called Sunday and yesterday, and she'd simply told him to leave her alone and hung up. Helen had instructions not to call her if he phoned again. She'd firmly refused to discuss the matter despite the woman's shocked protests.

She'd done her mourning, was desolate still, and knew that in a far corner of her feelings she'd mourn Cale for some time. But mourning it was. There were no options, no possibilities. For too long she'd sidestepped the growing evidence of what he'd made sickeningly clear Saturday night: his complete lack of regard for everything she was and did. That he still wanted to be with her was no surprise. He'd had almost everything he wanted and wasn't shy about trying to engineer the rest. He'd be happy to continue as they had been.

She was the one who had done all the changing. She'd become less abrupt and defensive. Her moods no longer zigzagged like a bad EKG. Early on he'd accused her of being too controlling; she'd tried to alter that too. In fact, she'd done such a good job, she saw now, that *he'd* gotten all the control.

You want me to redirect my career, Cale? Okay, I'll do improv. No good; that didn't work. I should make a movie now? Even though I hate the idea? Oops, sorry, I don't mean to be so controlling. Well, that didn't go either. Oh, you're going to throw me some crumbs? Let me open for Rana? And you'll even try and pretend comedy doesn't turn your stomach. Thank you, thank you.

Sandy was sweating though the sun wasn't that warm. She was doing what she'd sworn she wouldn't, going over the whole mess again. She'd been a dope for so long, not seeing the truth when it shouted in her ear.

Then you had to pull the doormat move of the year, didn't you, and beg to humiliate yourself right in his own club. You had to let things go that far, explode in your face, before all the signs you should have spotted before were clear.

She was crying again. She'd have thought there was nothing more in the reservoir.

You love someone and your intelligent mind dies like a frozen battery. Yes, Cale, I love you, Cale, what diabolical obstacle course can I run for you next, Cale?

179

The sun had gone in, and the rising wind was chapping her wet face, but still she sat. With so much agony inside, it hardly mattered if anything else hurt.

CHAPTER TEN

"Not to be personal," Rana said, joining Cale at the house table, "but I can't help noticing things are a little different around here the last week or so."

"Excuse me, will you? I don't feel like company."

"I can see that. And I'm going to ignore it."

Cale got up.

"Oh, don't be such a baby. You can stand to be hassled for five minutes. Five minutes, that's all, I promise. Then I'll go away and you can sulk in peace."

He shot her a look but took his chair again. "I don't want to talk about Sandy."

"Fine. I don't either." He glanced up. "I want to talk about you. What a fool you are to let her go, if that's what you're doing."

"Look, Rana, I'm running out of patience."

"Bull. You haven't had any to run out of. Quit glaring at me. I know I'm prying. It's my responsibility as a friend to pry."

"Can't you see I just want to forget the whole thing?"

"You don't look like a man who wants to forget. You look haunted."

He rubbed his eyes. It made them even redder.

"You must sleep about ten minutes a night. You're pale, your clothes don't match. You who always just walked out of a Brooks Brothers catalog. I'm not sure what happened but it doesn't take a mind reader to put together a picture."

She leaned toward him. "Sandy worked here for the first time last week. She had a rotten night. Then days go by and I don't see her, except through the window at Twinkles. You scowl at everybody and talk in grunts. What I think is, you gave her a hard time when it was the last thing she needed and she just won't take any more of that from you."

Cale met her eyes finally. "What do you mean, any *more?*"

"I mean the way you always put her down."

"What?" he asked, bewildered.

"Oh, Cale. Maybe you don't even realize it. You should see the difference between how you treat me or another singer, and Sandy."

He looked at her for a long minute. This wasn't what he thought he'd have to listen to before she'd leave him alone.

"You'd better explain," he said quietly.

"Well, it's so plain, I can't think how you'd miss it, but . . . see, you're full of compliments when I sing. Your face lights up. Anyone can see you love it. And in case I might not notice, you make sure and tell me. A good singing voice, a well-tuned instrument—that's all it takes to make Cale happy.

"But when Sandy or another comic goes on, you look like you're forcing yourself to sit there. If you say anything nice, it sounds like someone has a gun at your back. You always criticize some little thing about her act—her clothes, or a gesture, whatever. Any fool can see you're just picking because you plain don't like it."

Cale swallowed. It was difficult.

"I could never figure out," Rana said, frowning, "why Sandy took that. She sure isn't bashful. Sometimes she even made excuses for you. I was just starting to wonder if you had any idea how loved you were—that the lady would not only swallow her hurt, but pretend she wasn't *being* hurt—when you must have tipped her over the edge, and she started wondering some things too. Like what she needed this for." She studied his face. "Oh ho. There's someone home after all. I think I'm getting through."

Cale turned away. He felt suddenly naked.

"The part I don't get," Rana went on, "is *why* you don't like her act. Sandy's brilliant. And brave, wow! Think of the guts it takes to do what she does."

The word tunneled into his mind and sat there. *Guts.*

"So? I'm tired of doing all the talking. Say something."

Somehow that was the key to the whole thing. She dared, but he couldn't . . . and so he made it her fault. He buried his face in his hands and groaned.

"Cale?"

"It's my problem," he mumbled. "I took it out on her. Or on comedy. Both, I guess."

"I don't—"

"I never— I've had a hard enough time with my own career. Jazz, I mean."

"But you love jazz."

"Yes. But that's a tough row to hoe when your background, your whole orientation, is classical."

"Well, I know that about your background. I thought you just preferred jazz."

He chuckled without humor. "I wish it was that simple. It sounds funny from someone so far over twenty-one, but I grew up believing the only worthwhile music was classical. Now I know that isn't so, but . . . I guess in some way I'm still a hell of a snob. That means part of me has always been at war with the other part. And if I have a conflict about jazz, the thing I've devoted my career to, because I'm not sure it's worthwhile, well . . ."

"You must think comedy is lower than the pits."

"Yeah. I guess that is what I think. It's not art. It's just . . . frivolous."

The tabletop was wet from her glass of club soda, and Rana absently traced squiggles in the moisture. "That's what you really think? Or—"

"That's what the snob thinks. And there's something else." He grinned sadly. "The part I choke on when I'm not sleeping my ten minutes. I'm jealous."

"Oh?"

"I didn't know what I was jealous of, just that I was. But now I think I do. It's her guts."

"Why? You have guts. Keeping a club going takes a lot of courage. Your whole living is a risk."

"Maybe. But I'd never dare take the risks Sandy does, and deep down I hate myself for that. So much that I . . . I think I had to belittle her for daring to do what I couldn't."

"You mean you'd rather be a performer?"

He shrugged. "Wouldn't everyone who works in show business, really? Some have the guts and some don't. And the 'don'ts' hedge their bets. We keep ourselves safe by staying in management or some other sidelines area. I thought I was hot stuff twenty years ago when I picked Juilliard over the Boston Conservatory, where my father teaches. Big rebellious act. Went into jazz. Talent management, owning clubs. Okay, not bad. But what gives me the ulcer is"—he spread his hands on the table—"none of this is any great commitment compared to Sandy's. She's more committed to comedy than I've ever been to anything."

"If you don't mind my asking," Rana said, "what made her tell you to go jump? I assume there was some particular thing."

"I . . . said something unforgivable." He winced, remembering. Hot shame lanced through him. He'd give anything not to have said it. What had seemed at the time just a snipe like any other he now saw for the cruel dagger it was.

"It must have been a killer," Rana said softly, watching him.

"Yes."

"Have you tried apologizing?"

"I've been calling and calling. She won't even come to the phone."

"Does she know any of what you told me? About how it's your problem, and you took it out on her and everything?"

"No. I didn't know half of it myself until I put it together just now."

"I'm sure it'll make all the difference."

"You think so?"

"It would if it were me. Especially if I cared as much as Sandy does."

Cale pressed the bell again. He'd just had the door slammed in his face.

Sandy opened it with the chain on. "Go away!" she shouted through the two-inch opening.

"Will you please just listen a—"

"No! No! We have nothing to say to each other. What does it take for you to see that?"

"But there's something I want to—"

"Leave me alone! The only thing *I* want is to forget about you."

He clenched his teeth. "Please just—"

"Go *away!*" She banged the door shut with as much force as the small opening would allow.

"I was wrong!" he yelled at the closed door. A car had just pulled into the next driveway and a woman and a collie got out. They both gaped at him. In his frustration he didn't care. "Do you hear me?" he shouted louder. "I was wrong! Wrong!"

The collie came over and sniffed him. His mistress watched with a worried frown, as if afraid to antagonize this lunatic by calling the dog back.

"Open *up!* I need you!" He slammed the wood with the flat of his hand.

"Bella," the woman next door said softly.

"Sandy!"

The dog whimpered, sensing his distress. Cale automatically patted its head. This apparently was the last straw for the woman, who threw caution to the winds, hurried over, and pulled it back to safe ground.

"I don't bite unless I'm provoked," Cale told her. She ignored him and hustled the dog inside.

He rang the bell again. He waited. Nothing. He pressed it and kept his finger there. He knew it made a loud, annoying buzz no one could tolerate for long. The vibration hurt his finger, but still he kept up the pressure. Then suddenly the sound ceased. He strained his ears but it was definitely gone. His heart sank. She must have disconnected the mechanism where it rang in the kitchen.

He dropped his hand. He stood a moment, trying to think of something else he could do. There was nothing. His massive shoulders slumped, he went back to the Lincoln and drove away.

Sandy pushed open the door of Twinkles. Marcus Brawn saw her and came over. He kissed her cheek. "You're looking a little better."

"Better than what?"

"Oh, a week-old corpse. Listen, could you emcee the first show tonight?"

She sighed. She'd had trouble as it was mobilizing enough energy to do two sets on a rainy Saturday. "I thought you were emceeing."

"I'm supposed to. But a casting guy is coming to see me, and I'd rather have him watch me do a set. Virgil is acting like I tripped his grandmother. He won't let me go without exacting his ton of flesh unless I get someone good to replace me. Someone like"—he kissed her again—"you."

"Well, I'll do it, but you're going to wish you hadn't asked me. I'll probably drag everybody down. I'm not over my . . . cold."

Marcus looked shrewdly at her. She'd had the cold last week and was still using it to explain why she looked and acted like an extinct fish.

"You're a pro," he said. "You know you'll be good."

And, in truth, she did. There was a difference between Sandy in a happy mood and Sandy the performer playing a role; but only someone who knew her and show business intimately would spot it. She felt a sharp point of sadness as she pictured the one person who qualified. But she pushed it away. She had to gear up for the long evening ahead.

By nine thirty she felt ready to do a creditable imitation of a cheerful person. She opened the show by playing with the audience, not doing material yet. She got a sweet rhythm going. The room was full, but they were a friendly crowd, eager to laugh.

Even her one heckler was benign. "Did you stick your finger in a light socket?" he asked, referring to her hair, which was all ripples in the wet weather.

"No, do you recommend it?" she shot back, and while the audience chuckled she told them, "You can see he's taking this evening seriously. His socks match."

He said something else, she couldn't hear what, but it didn't matter. "Sir," she said, "I don't mind you having the last word, but I wish you'd get to it."

They loved that, and she used the crest of the laughter to bring up the first act.

The evening continued smoothly. It was a good lineup, and she had no trouble reestablishing the room's equilibrium after each act. The casting agent came in, Marcus did a great set, and Sandy was glad she'd been able to help.

She was introducing a singer when another heckler spoke from a corner of the room shadowed by the lights. She missed his words, and didn't want to encourage him by asking for a repeat, so she went on with her introduction. But the man persisted. Still she didn't hear. But she couldn't ignore him now. He had the audience's attention. They were waiting to see what she'd do.

"Could we have quiet in the back, please?" she said. "There are people up front here trying to sleep."

Again she tried to use the laughter to bring on the act, but it didn't work this time. The man wouldn't shut up. She tried once more to squelch him. "I'm at a loss for words," she told him. "I wish you were."

"Do I get a wish too? I wish you'd listen to me," the man said, and everything stood still. Now she knew why she couldn't understand him. Because Cale had been disguising his voice.

She opened her mouth, trusting it to spit forth something clever, the way it always did. But nothing happened. She stood frozen, in shock.

He said, "I want to tell you—"

"You have the right to remain silent," she inter-

189

rupted loudly, finding her voice again at last. "Why don't you do us all a favor and use it?"

The crowd laughed. Her stunned pause had barely been noticed. To them she was just sparring with some clown who thought he was funny. How could they know she was mobilizing every speck of cold courage she'd ever had to survive this?

"You have to let—"

"Hey, I don't want to say you've had one too many, but when you went to the men's room before, you knocked over two chairs and a waitress."

Cale had moved a little, into her line of vision, and she saw him cover his eyes with his hand. Humiliated? Too bad. Too damn bloody bad. The audience was still laughing, still unaware they were watching anything unusual. Good. If she could stand her ground, maybe he'd give up and go.

"I love you," he shouted. "I—"

"Oh, but I feel the same way. I have a special place in my heart for handicapped people."

The room grew quiet. His confession and her cutting put-down had finally made it clear that something was going on. Sandy's eyes began to burn. Please, please, no, she prayed. Let me keep my cool, let it not hurt yet, let me get out of this.

Cale pushed aside a chair and took a step closer to the stage. "I'm serious. And I'm going to keep saying what I came here to say until you run out of jokes."

"Then I hope you made a reservation for tomorrow night, because I'll still—"

"I love you!" he yelled again, loud enough to be heard in San Diego. "I keep trying to apologize.

You have to listen. What I said last week, the way I treated you, was unforgivable. But I hope you'll forgive me anyway."

The paralysis was back. No hot lines leaped up to save her. The next thing Sandy knew, Cale had gone through the small wing and come out onstage. He was next to her. The adored, familiar body . . . she didn't know what to. . . .

But he'd hurt her so! No matter what she'd said just now, how she'd tried to mortify him . . . if she kept at it all night, she couldn't wound him as he had her. He could never suffer as she had over him.

Could he?

She looked up. His face was full of pain. The kind of heavy, gray pain she'd begun to feel she was the only person ever to experience.

He took the mike from her hand. "You're a wonderful comic," he said into it. He turned to the rapt crowd. "Isn't she terrific?" The applause and cheers were deafening.

"I didn't appreciate you before because I was too busy being a jerk. A narrow, resentful, dumb jerk. But that's my problem, not yours. You're a spectacular talent. I want to watch you forever." With his free hand he caressed her cheek.

That was too much, the agony she saw in his face. His pain wasn't only as deep as hers—it *was* hers. Hot tears ran down her cheeks.

He took a breath. His hand, getting wet now, trembled on her skin. "Marry me, Sandy. And I want to manage you. That's what I have to give—let me give it to you."

Her eyes streamed harder. He was saying the

things she'd wished, hoped, longed to hear . . .
but never thought she would. He was telling her he
loved her in all the ways she wanted him to—for all
she was and did.

"Do it!" the audience was shouting.

"Yes!" she screamed, and the mike clattered to
the floor as Cale clasped her in his arms and the
crowd went wild.